The Austrian Painter: What if Germany won the Great War?

The Austrian Painter: What if Germany won the Great War?

—

William Stroock

ISBN-13: 9781981431861
ISBN-10: 1981431861

Part I

CHAPTER 1

IT IS A WARM AUGUST morning and I leave my small flat overlooking the River Spree with easel, canvas, paint and pallet packed in an old case. Slightly hunched over I walk along Friedrichstrasse. I pass all the sites and places made familiar during my decades here. I know most of the shopkeepers and street vendors; they wave and smile to me. Many have been doing so since they were children. Here and there a stranger looks on at my 75-year-old visage. One well-meaning young woman asks if I need help. I decline politely and ask if she would like a portrait, perhaps for her boyfriend? Feeling sorry for me, I think, she agrees. I take out my sketch book and she sits down on a planter. She says she is new to Berlin and she is studying at Humboldt University. Her father is worried and wouldn't a sketch of herself in her new surroundings soothe him?

Her name is Ilse, a pretty young thing with a full face, blue eyes and long, brown hair. She is dressed in the latest nouveau clothes from England that I have seen many of the young people wear. I ask Ilse what it is called, she says 'Mod', whatever that means. Ilse tells me she is from Bavaria, which I realize as soon as she speaks, her accent is most thick, and this warms my heart; a country girl in Europe's great metropolis. Ilse says she has been here for three weeks. As I add accents to her hair, I ask Ilse how she finds Berlin. It is intimidating, she says, but exciting too; the people, the air, the electricity. I smile to myself. By then I have finished the sketch. I hand it to Ilse and she says her father will like it very much. She gives me a five *reichsmark* note. I nod and thank her.

I continue down the street till I come to Weder's Café where for years I have read the papers over a morning cup of tea. The nice middle-aged couple that own the café have my table ready with a cup and a selection of teabags and copies of my preferred paper, *Der Spiegel Taglich.* I sit at the small round table and pour myself a cup of tea.

I look at the paper's front page. <u>50 Years of Peace!</u> declares the 10-centimeter-high headline. *Forty-nine* years, I say to myself. I know. In 1915 I was in the east being shot at and shelled by Russians. But I understand *Spiegel's* sentiment. The great powers have not gone to war since 1914. Oh, there's been a few small conflicts, and the Habsburg Question of the 1920's and all the European powers have colonial police actions to deal with including Germany's own Congo Crisis. But even with the French agitating for a war of revenge and the Russian menace to the east we have maintained the peace.

'Guten tag!' says Frau Weder as she waters the flower boxes in the front window.

I wave and smile.

Herr Weder comes out. He is something of a news aficionado and always wants to discuss events with me. This morning the topic is trouble in the Reich's Congo colony.

'Mobutu strikes again,' he says.

'Ah.'

I turn over the front page of *Der Spiegel* and indeed there is a headline about Mobutu's rebels attacking a power station in Goma.

Weder asks, 'What do you think?'

Weder assumes that because of my age and experience I know everything. This is especially so regarding the Congo because I once visited the place on an artist's commission. I shrug, 'I never traveled that far into Congo,' I reply. I point to Goma on the map provided by *Der Spiegel's* editors. It is clear across the colony. 'I don't think I ever went further than a few hundred kilometers up the Congo. That was far enough, believe me.'

'Johann!' calls Frau Weder. 'The grill!'

'Excuse me,' Herr Weder says.

I suspected Frau Weder is calling Herr Weder away so he will leave me to my tea and newspaper. I laugh to myself and read on. Aside from the news out of Congo, it is always in the paper these last few years. *Der Spiegel* is going on about the latest maneuverings in the Reichstag. 'Legislation Introduced to Curb Imperial Prerogative' declares one headline. I scoff. Old Kaiser Wilhelm would never stand for such a thing. 'Abolition of Royal Prerogative Proposed,' reads the sub-headline. Another headline reads, 'Chancellor Speer Open to Talks'. I scoff again. If they could, the SPD reformers would abolish the Kaiser altogether. Unthinkable! Wilhelm III seems indifferent to these machinations, though the young adventurer crown prince has embraced the SPD, when he has time between safaris and mountain climbing jaunts. The SPD has made trouble since before the Great War. I move on to the international news, seismic tremors in French Polynesia, the machinations of the Russian premier, and the like.

I finish my paper and tea and walk inside Weder's. The interior is small with one counter opposite the small kitchen and another counter lining the great picture window overlooking the sidewalk. Several of my paintings hang within. They are for decoration and sale and I make a modest income from the paintings sold here. Several of my postcards line the lavatory walls. These depict scenes around Berlin, the Tiergarten, the Reichstag, the Kaiser Memorial. As the café does get some tourist business, I usually sell a few postcard bundles every week. After costs I split the proceeds with the Weders.

I say goodbye to the Weders and walk over to the Unter den Linden. The street and its medians are filling up with people. I proceed west down the Unter den Linden toward the Brandenburg Gate. Beyond that, one can see the mighty Kaiser Wilhelm Statue, standing forty meters high and looking down upon the capitol of the mighty empire he made. He is ringed by statues of his great ministers and generals. Hindenburg stands slightly higher, of course, and other great generals like Moltke and Falkenhayn, Bethmann-Hollweg and Zimmermann, the greatest European diplomat since Metternich they say. As I look past the gate down the 17 Juni Strasse, most of the people are tourists. As well they would be.

Today I will do well. Just look at all the eager people. The keen eye sees three types of tourists. First, Germans from all points between the Rhine and the Elbe. These are well kept and orderly, of course, and their faces reveal little. As this is Victory Week, I see Germans arriving from points in the empire as well. Some are tanned by the African sun. Others have acquired a bit of Chinese flair to their dress - their wives wear a high collar, their children seem to prefer loose slacks and long shirts. I see one man wearing an opened collar tropical shirt. He is accompanied by a Polynesian wife, perhaps he is a sugar planter from the South Seas?

Second, one sees English tourists. In recent decades, the English have developed a kind of morbid fascination with the Reich which has built an economy, currency and empire to rival their own. Between them the great German and British empires rule half the earth. Though our two nations fought one another in the Great War, we are long reconciled. After all, the Great Kaiser Wilhelm was himself half an Englishman and it seemed odd for two of Victoria's grandsons to battle one another, notwithstanding her other grandson, the unfortunate Czar Nicholas. Walking about the Tiergarten and standing in the shadow of the Kaiser Statue the Englishman doesn't quite know what to make of Teutonic greatness.

Thirdly, one sees the Americans. They mean well, one supposes, and I have met many not only with German names, but with German-speaking parents and grandparents in tow. But for the most part the Americans are crude and loud. They talk over everyone and everything. They are physically loud too, with their Hawaiian vacation shirts and their shorts and their tennis shoes. And they are big. The men all seem as if they are trying out for their bastardized version of football. And they are energetic. Their children run to and fro, knocking over other children and often interfering with my own work. Even if the American parents could control their children, they do not do so.

But I stomach the Americans. They are the biggest spenders and will pay ten reichsmarks for a sketch of their children standing before the Brandenburg Gate. Often that won't do. Many times an American family will ask me to take their photograph for them. The first time this happened I demanded a mark and to my astonishment the father paid. So whenever an American asks me to take a photograph I demand a mark, and they pay. Very often this gives me an opening to show them some post cards and usually I can sell a few. For the most part the Americans lack artistic sense, except for their Hudson River School and the American west. I know, I have seen both places with my own eyes. So the Americans prefer their cameras and do not see the irony in the proliferation of Japanese cameras. Despite the bitter and brutal war between the two nations, the Americans simply do not care.

The Americans' English cousins look on in wry amusement and they look knowingly at me as if to say, 'Dumb Americans'. I do not mean to speak ill of the Americans, the Yanks as my English patrons call them. For I have visited their country and it is great. And if the American is uncouth at least he is friendly. Such openness. Such optimism. I suppose when one's nation is not constantly consumed with the eternal Russian threat, one can afford to be happy.

Which is more than one can say for my fellow Berliners. Of course, cynical and hard-bitten Berliners stay away from the Brandenburg Gate, only coming here themselves when entertaining visitors. Universally this is a chore. But not to me. I enjoy being around this architectural greatness to Frederick the Great and old Prussia, the neo-classical archways and columns harkening back to classical Greece and ancient Rome.

I set up my easel and canvas, then a rack with a dozen hand-painted Berlin post cards - two marks each. With the throngs of Americans here today I am sure to sell most if not all I have on hand. But the real money comes from the portraits. I begin a sketch of the crowd. Today the people are more interesting than usual. Many are carrying commemorative flags. Some enterprising businessman has pressed commemorative T-shirts, and of course the Americans purchase and wear these. I admit the design is interesting. In this case it is a Prussian soldat of the 1871 War followed by a German soldat from the Great War followed by a modern German soldat. Judging by his camouflage fatigues this soldat serves in the Congo.

'Hello there,' says a man with two sons. 'Can you do our portrait?'

'Ja, Ja,' I reply.

The father wears a simple button-down shirt. The two boys look to be about seven and five and are both wearing those Wehrmacht commemorative T-shirts.'

'Ja, ja,' I say, 'Stand in front of the gate so it is in the background.'

'Oh right, of course.'

As I make the sketch I attempt small talk. It turns out these are not Americans, but Canadians and they are here for Victory Week.

When I finish, I show the sketch to the boys, who are delighted. The father reaches into his pocket. 'How much?'

I hold up five fingers. He gives me a five reichsmark note. This is one of the new notes, marking fifty years of German military achievement. The great Hindenburg adorns the front and I am glad as the treasury used the portrait made by my old friend Hugo Vogel. There he is, Hindenburg, his face a determined mask of steel, eyes looking off page toward the crisis, his head framed by the collar of his great coat. Vogel sketched the famous piece in early 1915, Hindenburg looks east as did all Germany then. A year later Hindenburg stood triumphant on the banks of the Volga, but at that time all Germany looked east with trepidation. Vogel's interpretation really shows it. The English tourists see the image of Hindenburg on the note and look on with admiration. They fear the Russian bear too. Of course the Americans have no idea who adorns the note and do not want to know. One senses that the Americans believe no general could compare to their heroes of the Great Pacific War, Stilwell and MacArthur.

The day passes quickly and well. By lunch all of my postcards are gone and I have made three more sketches, two for English customers one for Americans. At one o'clock I pack up my easel and paints and eat a quick, simple vegetarian lunch. In old age my stomach can handle little else. I observe and enjoy the crowd. By the time I finish my lunch the gate is thick with people and the sun is hot. It is too crowded for me. I pick up my bag and begin the walk home. Many of the tourists see an old man seemingly struggling with a burden across his shoulders. Most look on sympathetically. A few stop me and ask if I need assistance. These are usually Americans. Why do Americans think that speaking loudly will make them better understood? Sometime you will get one who speaks horribly broken German. This is actually worse. The Americans mean well, bless them. I always keep my head down and respond with a curt, 'Nein'. I do not need them. I have walked far greater distances with far heavier burdens, though that was fifty years ago.

I return to my flat. It is in a nondescript apartment building along the Spree. An entryway, bedroom, bath, kitchen and drawing room which is my studio. Here I have lived for over a decade. The walls I have covered with prints collected from all over the world. My bedroom is small and lined with shelves. Upon these rest the works of Schopenhauer, Kant and Nietzsche, as well as my precious Karl May novels and few other fiction writers, historians and current events prognosticators. I read a few favored and comforting passages of Schopenhauer before lying down. Then I nap my customary two hours.

I wake up refreshed and ready for my nightly foray out.

It is Tuesday and my favorite television program airs at seven. I do not own a television. I have never had much use for one as I find the German programs to be heavy-handed and the ones imported from America utter trash, except for the occasional airing of a Disney film or an American western.

As I dress the phone rings. It is Otto, 'Mein Herr,' Otto says. 'Your program airs in twenty minutes.'

'Ja, ja,' I say.

My entire life I have been unable to be punctual. Otto's phone call is his way of ensuring I am on time. In the cooling off air of the evening I walk down to Otto's. Because I knew the owner's father during the war, Otto reserves a seat for me at a small table before the television set. When I walk in, Otto is wiping down the bar and waves. At forty years of age, he is the image of his father - short, rotund with a large flat face. He is aging the same way as well, becoming rounder with each year. Otto's has been my 'watering hole' as the cowboys might say for many, many years. I am afraid as those years pass Otto's is becoming something of an anachronism. The once stately furniture shows year upon year of dink and dent. The large Dortmunder Lager mirror behind the bar is chipped. Time has taken its toll on the dark oak wall paneling.

Last year an entire panel slid off the wall, falling on a young man and his girlfriend, a scene I must admit I very much enjoyed. I am afraid the youth of Berlin is starting to enjoy Otto's because it has, as one young woman described to me, 'a pre-war feel.' Indeed that is what Otto was striving for, but not in the way this young fraulein meant it. Modern Germany has seen an outburst of minimal, brutalist architecture, much concrete and angles giving new buildings a utilitarian sheen. These youth have grown up surrounded by the brutalist look, and I think they enjoy Otto's rundown and shabby feel. Their attire matches Otto's. If I had carried myself in such a way, my dear mother would have cried. Gone are the crisp, clean clothes of my youth. Young people today enjoy British style clothes or American-made blue jeans, t-shirts, baggy sweaters and those awful shoes American basketball players wear. These young men keep their hair in a state of disaster. This is just disgraceful. Frankly I wonder if the Congo Crisis is not a good thing for this generation. I have tried to appreciate these young people as they intrude on Otto's. After all, I was once a Vienna Bohemian myself, but these youths are trying my patience. As I sit in the same place nearly every day the young people assume that I am the owner and my name is in fact, 'Otto'.

I sit before the television. Otto greets me and brings a cup of tea and a piece of chocolate cake. He turns on the television just as the evening game show is ending. I loathe this kind of program, and I have often wondered if Kaiser Wilhelm would have stomached their airing. His grandson doesn't seem to mind and even says he is a big fan of American game shows. Utter tripe.

While we in the Reich are celebrating the 50th anniversary of our Great War, the Americans are celebrating the 20th anniversary of their victory over the Japanese in the Great Pacific War. In the American mind this means parades, flags and fireworks and it did not seem to occur to anyone in New York, Los Angeles or even Washington to produce a tele-documentary about the war. Instead the task has fallen to the BBC. Since Britain has no war to commemorate, and hasn't been involved in a European conflict since the Great War, the BBC has taken it upon itself to graciously produce a massive documentary series on the Great Pacific War, almost as if they are sorry Britain did not participate in the conflict.

The credits roll and then the screen goes blank. I blush to admit that I wait for the program with child-like anticipation. Then I hear drums and rising music and suddenly in large block letters the words, 'The Pacific War' appear on the screen. Dramatic music begins as a series of photographs run across the screen; a smoldering *USS Arizona*, Japanese troops fighting their way into Honolulu, the famous photograph of the American battleship line hammering their Japanese counterparts at the Battle of Panama Gulf, an American soldier clad in snow camouflage in the Aleutians campaign, MacArthur's landing on

Maui, and finally a haunting photo of a gaunt, almost skeleton-like Japanese family after the Great Starvation.

The credits fade and a subtitle comes on screen, 'Episode Seven: Retaking Hawaii and across the Pacific.' This episode is quite interesting, first with Admiral Halsey's following up his great victory at the Gulf of Panama by inflicting a debilitating defeat at the Battle of Hilo. Then General MacArthur landed his army on the Big Island and began the liberation of Hawaii. After spending three weeks clearing the Big Island he made his next landing on Oahu. The Japanese fought for every block of Honolulu and by the time they won the battle the Americans had nothing more to show for it than a great pile of rubble. Fifty thousand people were killed in the melee.

Behind me two young men hoot and holler at the TV. I have been waiting for this episode about the American liberation of Hawaii and do not want to be disturbed. I turn from the television and hiss at the two boys. This time my mistaken identity serves me well, they quiet down for 'Otto'.

In 1942 the Marshalls, Carolines and Marianas all fell, and a series of naval engagements sunk a half dozen Japanese aircraft carriers in exchange for a half dozen American aircraft carriers. The difference is that with its economy now fully mobilized, the Americans could make good their losses while the Japanese could not. In 1943 alone the Americans brought six new carriers into the Pacific and another ten in 1944. That year MacArthur led a massive invasion of the Philippines while Stilwell came down from the Aleutians and hit Okinawa. These battles led to frightful slaughter on both sides and forced the Willkie Administration to think of ways other than invasion to end the war...

As episode seven fades to black, on comes the evening news. The broadcast leads with celebration preparations in Berlin and other cities. From there the anchor moves on to domestic news, the daily update on the Kaiser, politics in the Reichstag and such. The screen fades and leads to a series of television commercials. These sell Volkswagens and cheap trips to Greece. The anchor returns.

'Today in Congo, German troops rounded up several men with suspected ties to the terrorist Mobutu. Meanwhile in Wilhelmsville, a bomb exploded, wounding two Congolese policeman and destroying a municipal bus. No one was killed...'

Having no desire to watch the morbid and the fluff of the news broadcast I leave a few reichmarks on the bar and excuse myself.

'See you tomorrow...' Otto says.

I walk back to my flat where I spend the next several hours in my studio. On this evening I am working on a grand vista of the Unter den Linden, not in the present day but in 1916.

Here we see row on row of German soldaten clad in gray and black, rifles carried on the shoulder, bayonets gleaming in the autumn sun. At the head of each regiment the commander rides atop a horse, behind him come two other horsemen, each carrying the proud unit banner and the flag of the Iron Cross. Each regiment goes through the Brandenburg Gate and then past a massive review stand. Here waits the Kaiser of course, flanked on one side by the great Moltke the Younger, and the other by the even greater Hindenburg. They watch almost impassively as regiment after regiment marches by. It was the grandest display these eyes have ever looked upon. Historians say it was the greatest victory parade since the American's Grand Review commemorating their Civil War in 1865. During my own trip to the American West all those years ago, I was curious and asked a librarian in El Paso if they had any pictures of that event. She found me a book of Mathew Brady photographs and sure enough, there were dozens from the Americans' Grand Review. Splendid in blue, the American army marched down their own Constitution Avenue past a reviewing stand. The scene is indeed great, though the American capital in 1865 lacked the splendor of Berlin in 1916.

Now I paint my own interpretation. For a few days I am having trouble with the reviewing stand. The picture-scape is vast and it is difficult to show the three great men at a distance. Right now, to my eye Kaiser, Chief of Staff and General are lost in a vast sea of gray and black. I would like to delineate Hindenburg, perhaps with a little red about the collar. This I find risky though, as Vogel always told me how meticulous Hindenburg was about being portrayed in the proper uniform down to the buttons. I want to be respectful towards the architect of our great victory against Russia.

In frustration I go to my art bookshelf and take out a collection of Vogel's prints. I flip through until I find the print I am looking for...ah there it is. Vogel's *Hindenburg on the Vistula, Victory at Vilnius*. The great Hindenburg stands on the crest of a hill, the river and city off to his left. Further in the distance on the right the Russian army marches forward unknowingly to its destruction. This is of course only the first of Vogel's three renowned works, each portraying one of Hindenburg's trio of victories in 1915.

I spend another hour or so working on the grand victory painting. When finished, I shower and dress for bed. Though it is late I am not really tired and look for a book to read. I pick *Asia at Twenty*, about the development of Asia and the Pacific Rim since the war. With the reemergence of Japan and the development of China under the KMT the author posits that Asia will dominate the 21st Century.

With my eyelids finally heavy I put the book down and close my eyes. Given the war anniversary and the preparations engulfing the city, seeing my friend's work now takes me back, a bit of unusual nostalgia. After all, I was in the east with Hindenburg, though it took some time for me to get there as I began the war in the west...

CHAPTER 2

1914

——

LIKE MOST GERMANS IN 1914, I was enthusiastic about the war. Finally Germany would have its rightful place: first in the European community of nations. To this day I recall the great rally at the Munich Odeonsplatz. How I cheered! Later, after some negotiation with the authorities I enlisted in the Bavarian army and was assigned eventually to the 16th Reserve Infantry Regiment. We spent the early months of the war at barracks in Munich before being ordered to Lechfeld outside of Augsburg. Here our regimental commander, Colonel Julius List, took us through excruciating training. This entailed daily marches sometimes over 30 kilometers, rifle practice, as well as regimental and brigade level drills. In this way we learned how to be soldiers.

Our training came under the stern tutelage of Sgt. Ammon. Always he was exhorting, yelling, screaming, beating us into competent soldiers. He would do so throughout the war.

We volunteers hailed from all over Bavaria. Our ranks included many farmers and a few fellow artists, including the commander of 1st Company, Lt. Albert Weisgerber. I did not then know his impressionist work. He was tall and lanky, with a thin, high-cheeked face and dirty blond hair. Till the end of his life, Lt. Weisgerber travelled in powerful circles within the German arts and political community. But in 1914 he was just another officer in the 16th RIR. I have always thought well of him and been thankful he was our company commander. We also had in our ranks one Captain Julius von Zech, former governor of the Reich's Togo colony. We were not all a merry band though. We had in the ranks some unsavory and downright criminal types. Mostly, though, we were a lot of men new to the army. Dressed in gray we

14

were, with a red stripe running down our trousers, these tucked into brand new leather boots. Our 16th RIR unit insignia was sewn into our epaulettes. Atop our heads we wore a flat cap with a red badge in front. We carried the Mauser 1898. Frankly I was not much of a marksman.

During these early weeks my greatest fear was that the war would end before I got in it. As events progressed my fear was well justified. First the Wehrmacht beat the French on the Marne. From there our victories came quickly. These were a series of successful actions to get across the Seine, the boxing out of the English outside Paris and finally the furious battle to get across the Loire. By the time the 16th RIR's training was complete, tens of thousands of German troops were south of Paris and threatening to completely envelope the city. Our own forces were between the capital and what was left of the French army, which neared collapsed. Understanding that nothing could save Paris, the English withdrew to the north in good order so as to defend the Channel.

In early October, Colonel List told us to be ready to move out. I packed my few meager belongings, Schopenhauer books and sketch pad, in a rucksack and waited. For days around the camp field we speculated, would we be shipped to the west or to the east? On 21 October we received our answer. The 16th RIR boarded a trio of trains and departed for points west. I for one was excited. A few days later, I lay eyes upon the River Rhine for the first time. Not till I spied the mighty Hudson River a few years later would I see a river so impressive. Our train ran along its banks through Köln and Aachen. Then we entered Belgium, this was our first sight of war. We passed train stations shot to pieces, and several towns reduced to rubble.

The 16th RIR disembarked at Lille. Here is where the war hit home for me. We saw thousands upon thousands of Belgian and French refugees with no place to go. Then we saw the French prisoners. Thousands of wretched, seemingly lost souls. In hastily built camps they milled about without purpose. We passed thousands more marching along the road. It seemed almost comical to see a hundred men guarded by just a few German soldiers. But these Frenchmen were defeated. I saw it in their long faces and forlorn eyes, their shiftless gaits and tattered uniforms. For fifty years I have thanked god that I did not know the defeat these Frenchman suffered. Along the road from behind barbed wire they watched us march, fearing for their own homes and families. This angered me greatly. We were not brutes like the Russians. Word of Russian atrocities against the German people was widely circulated and many of us burned with anger. With the war in the west more or less settled we were anxious to move east to defend the fatherland.

The sight of our own German soldiers surprised me and many of my comrades in the List Regiment. I expected strong, stout soldiers singing songs of victory. Instead our own men looked more ragged than the French prisoners. Later I understood why from my own experience. They were in the field longer, many wearing the same uniform from the Rhine to the Seine. Even taking this into account, our men had the same weary look as their French counterparts, young men of 18 or 19 seemingly aged ten years.

Once we stopped along the road as a *landwehr* regiment was coming back east, I cannot recall which. They began the war with 1,600 men, but were coming home with barely five hundred in their ranks. I briefly chatted with a youngster who asked for a cigarette. I did not smoke but my friend Ernst Schmidt did. The young soldier had seemingly aged ten years in two months with worry lines across his face and gray in his hair. I asked the young soldier where he had been. As he drew deeply on his cigarette he replied only, 'All over.'

'The Marne?' I asked. 'The Seine? The Loire?'

He replied only, 'Ja,' He thanked Schmidt for the cigarette and went on his way.

As the young soldier's regiment moved on, I reached into my haversack and took out my sketch book. I cursed myself, wishing that I had asked the man to remain so that I could make a quick drawing of him. In retrospect now I realize it would have been foolish for me to ask such a thing of him. In a few months I would also understand why he would not tell me about his travails at the front.

My first encounters with the realities of war gave me pause, sobered me even as to the true nature of war. Still we were disappointed at being kept out of the fighting, as was Colonel List. The Colonel did much to soothe the regiment, he explained to us, as it was no doubt explained to him that by occupying Lille we freed up other forces for action in France.

That campaign was coming to fruition. Throughout the cold and rainy month of October our forces worked their way around and behind Paris until by the end of the month the French capital was boxed in on three sides. As Von Kluck's First Army readied to seal the box, authorities within declared Paris an open city. The French government attempted to intervene, but already having fled to Bordeaux, they had little moral sway against the Parisian authorities who were trying to spare the city a repeat of the disastrous siege of the last war. Our own forces marched into Paris on 1 November. For the first few days of December we of the List Regiment wondered if and when we would move north to fight the English. The BEF was now far removed from Paris and centered on Rouen to protect the Channel ports. It seemed logical that we would move out to engage them, but it was not to be. Understanding that France was on its own, on 5 December the Bordeaux government asked for a cessation of hostilities. The Kaiser agreed. In this effort both sides were assisted by the American President Woodrow Wilson, who dispatched his close confidant, Colonel House, to act as liaison between the two sides and negotiate a final peace settlement.

We remained in Lille throughout December. It was a dull time of daily street patrols. There seems to have been a general agreement by the people of Lille to limit interaction with the German occupier. Getting a citizen of Lille to say hello or even acknowledge your presence was difficult. We had little but time and I used mine as best I could. I read and re-read my Schopenhauer. I walked the city of Lille taking in its art museums and architecture, fortunately these were untouched by the war. Like all great French cities Lille had its share of cathedrals. Of all these the Eglise St. Maurice was the most impressive. Inside, the stained glass windows were an extraordinary work of art. I spent an afternoon here sketching the exterior and then the interior.

I did not tour the city alone, doing so was too dangerous. I went around the city with Schmidt and half dozen of my comrades. I could never stay at the cathedral or any other landmark as long as I wished. Always my comrades wanted to move on, preferably to an ale house. The French barkeeps may have resented Germany's victory, but our money was still good with them. More than once I was trying to finish a sketch only to have an insistent and impatient fellow soldier tug at my sleeve and tell me to hurry up. At least there were plenty of sketch subjects at the ale houses. In one a handlebar-mustached owner allowed me to sketch him outside of his establishment, arms folded, with his face holding a look of defiance. Many times I sketched my comrades at the bar enjoying an ale or whisky or wine. Their overcoats were slung over their chairs, collars loosened, faces displaying a look of relief as they enjoyed their drinks and perhaps ogled the occasional French barmaid.

There were many architectural sites as well. One by one I sketched these and even had the time and resources to paint a few watercolors. They were good and included one of our intrepid leader, Colonel List. This watercolor along with the few others I was able to paint remain with me. It is a sentimental reminder of what turned out to be the calm before the storm. Today my watercolor of Colonel List sits on my fireplace mantel, a gentle reminder of a special time in my life. I am proud to say that much of my work later went into the regimental history published in 1932.

That special time came to an end just before Halloween. Word came that we were moving out. Colonel List did not know precisely where we were going, just that our regiment, along with dozens of others, was heading east.

Ours was a long train ride back through Germany. The journey's sites were not what I expected. Instead of a nation ebullient with victory we saw a countryside riven with great trepidation. Even after Hindenburg's great victory at Tannenberg, the Czar had vast armies on the frontier. Germany was awash with stories of atrocities by beastly Russian troops in the east. Today these atrocities are the stuff of legend and they come up again in the Reichstag whenever the SPD proposes funding reductions for Das Vistula Corps.

Ours was one of countless trains heading east to confront the Russian beast. The need was so great, and the tracks so choked that many times our train moved at a crawl. More than once we were stopped on the tracks for hours. One day after midnight we passed through Berlin. Most of my comrades slept, but I couldn't. How I wished to detrain to see the great sites of the capital, to take in its museums and architectural wonders. I actually burned as our train moved through the city. It was a young man's lust, though at 25 I should have known better. To try to experience a city like Berlin in a day. . . foolishness. Even writing about the desire, fifty years later, fills me with embarrassment.

By dawn we were through the city. The car was filled with chatter of course. Men spoke of the future, or ale, or women; on and on about women. Frankly I have always thought such constant obsession was bad for the psyche and the body. Here again Schopenhauer knows best. I was trying to ignore one of my comrade's wholly unrealistic tale of sexual conquest when Lt. Weisgerber came into the car. Right now, we were about to learn, it was time celebrate.

'Men,' he said, 'I have an announcement.'

Collective groaning filled the car.

Lt. Weisgerber banged his walking stick on the floor until we quieted down. 'Men, the war in the West is over!'

Now uproarious cheers filled the car, some hooted and whistled, my comrades shook the windows, they were so loud. 'This evening the French and Belgian delegations agreed to the terms demanded by the Kaiser.'

We gave a great cheer. Schmidt asked, 'What did we get?'

Lt. Weisgerber looked at the note. 'All it says is that France and Belgium have agreed to terms. It's called the Treaty of Strasbourg.' A clever name, I thought, as this invoked the great Charlemagne.

Schmidt again asked, 'What did we get?'

'There is nothing in here about what we received.'

I asked, 'What about Britain?'

Lt. Weisgerber looked at the piece of paper. 'The note says nothing about Britain.'

'So we are still at war.'

'Yes, Private, we are still at war with Great Britain.'

Indeed we were and in 1915 while we battled Russia, Britain would reclaim its national honor. That still lay a year away and when it did happen the Chancellor convinced the Kaiser to ignore Britain and rest on the laurels of Germany's great victory. By then Wilhelm II was the greatest German leader since at least Frederick. Some even called him the Barbarossa of the 20th Century and even compared him to Charlemagne. But in January 1915 Wilhelm II's victory was only half complete. His Roncesvalles lay in the future and I am proud to say I and the 16th Reserve Infantry Regiment played a part in it...

CHAPTER 3

1964

———

THIS MORNING AT WEDER'S MY tea and newspapers await me as always. The headline in *Der Spiegel* is a bit troubling: <u>Two White Farms Burned in Katanga Province Farmers killed, wives and children missing.</u> The paper helpfully provides a map, showing Katanga province in the southern part of the Congo. I read on and the facts here are gruesome. Just thinking about what Mobutu's savages would do with the poor farmers' wives makes me angry.

Herr Weder points to the paper and says, 'I cannot believe what those jungle schwartzes did.'

'Mmmm...' I reply as I read on.

One of the families was German, the other Belgian, Flemish judging by the name.

'We should burn down all their nearby villages.'

I have long learned to ignore Herr Weder's martial bluster. Though the newspaper article does not say so, those farms were most likely plantations reliant on local labor. Burning down the local villages would help no one and only drive the locals into Mobutu's arms.

Herr Weder would like to go on but Frau Weder stops him.

She says to me, 'We have an offer for one of your paintings.'

'Oh, wonderful, I say. Which one?'

'*Karlskirche, Vienna.*'

'Ahhhh, of course,' I say.

I have forgotten how many times in my career I have sold that painting. Though the *Karlskirche* in Vienna is an old baroque masterpiece, in my own work I emphasized the lines and columns in a way that almost makes the 18th century design look stark and neo-classical. I repaint the piece at least once per year.

'Two hundred marks.'

I raise my eyebrows. We were asking two-seventy-five.

Frau Weder has an eye for business, Herr Weder merely works at the café, though he does not realize it. I trust Frau Weder's judgement implicitly.

'We should accept the offer,' she advises.

'Then we shall.'

Of late a wave of nostalgia for the old Habsburg empire has come over Germany. More than 40 years have passed since the empire fell apart in one violent, empire-wide convulsion. When Kaiser Wilhelm wisely refused to send troops to quell the rebellion, Charles I, 'The Last Emperor' as he is known, wisely declared the dissolution of the empire.

After tea I make my way along the Unter den Linden. This day will also be hot. I take my easel and pallet down to the Brandenburg Gate. It is a bit more crowded than the previous day. More tourists, more visitors. In five minutes I sell a postcard to a young man on honeymoon with his bride.

'I promised my grandmother I would send her a postcard from the old country,' he tells me.

'Ah,' I smile. 'Old country. Your grandmother is German then?'

He is American and tells me his name is Gortkey. I wince at the bastardization of a fine German name and correct him on the pronunciation. He laughs and tells me how his grandfather, from Bavaria it turns out, used to correct him. Gortkey tries to impress with the few German sentences his grandfather taught him. Indeed he does speak with a Bavarian accent. Gortkey's young bride comes over and chides him for taking too long with me.

Our young Gortkey is lucky. His bride is voluptuous and blonde, almost the epitome of idealized German femininity.

'Excuse me?' I interject out of curiosity, 'May I ask your maiden name, young lady?'

'Murphy,' she says curtly.

'Ah, so Irish then?'

'My grandfather was from Cork.'

'Oh, how lovely,' I say.

'He never thought so.'

'Oh?'

'He left after the English hung Collins and de Valeria.'

I try to get back to business. 'Mrs. Gortkey. How would the young bride like a honeymoon sketch? As a memento?'

'I am sorry, I...'

'A keepsake, miss. For your grandchildren?'

She blushes, 'Well...'

'It will only take a moment.'

As they always do, the young woman agreed.

In ten minutes I sketch the happy couple, posing arm in arm before the Brandenburg Gate. Five reichsmarks easily made.

'If you would like more sketches, please come back.'

'Thank you, sir...'

I click my heels and bow most properly, 'At your service, sir.'

Americans love that.

On the walk home I stop by Fredo's newsstand down the street from Weder's.

I peek through the art section but see none of the architectural magazines I read. Disappointed, I move to the automotive section but this too is filled with old editions I have already read over. Fredo comes waddling over. He is a fat man, morbidly so, and I believe he owns the newsstand so he can sit on a stool all day and talk with passersby. He is friendly though and stocks my favorite magazines.

'Good afternoon.'

'Still nothing?' I ask.

'I am getting a shipment from the distributor tomorrow.'

'So, there is a good chance my magazines will be among them?'

'Ja, come back tomorrow.'

I walk away in resignation. I am eager to see reviews of the latest American models.

Once home I draw a bath and cleanse myself of the day's work. Afterwards I feel refreshed and ready for the afternoon nap.

Unfortunately, people are in the hallway, which is unusual for this time of day. As I lay down I notice they keep coming and going. They chatter - the quick, loud chatter of young men without respect for those of us trying to enjoy quiet. Unable to put the noise out of my mind, I hear every bump, every stumble. I rise, put on a robe, and open the door.

In the hallway are two young men wrestling with a large cabinet. The cabinet is winning.

'What is this commotion?' I ask.

One of the men turns around. He is large and muscle-bound with the broadest shoulders I have ever seen. Atop those shoulders sits a large, square head framed by a buzzed haircut. Instantly I think of him as 'the Dumb One'.

It is the other young man who speaks, confirming my assessment. 'Apologies, mein Herr,' he says most politely.

This one is tall and lanky with spindly, sinewy arms. Though thin and angular, this one's face shares characteristics of the Dumb One's face, the shape of the eyes and nose, the protruding chin. They are brothers, and he must be the 'Smart One'.

The Smart One says, 'We are movers.'

'I see,' I say. At least the commotion is justified.

'We will try not to disturb you, mein Herr,' he says with great deference.

Mollified, I hold up a hand, 'Ja, ja. Just go about your job, young man.'

I am about to close the door when I see the Smart One's hand running down his arm tracing a long, red scar with just a hint of purple. I stay and watch as the movers manhandle the cabinet into the apartment down the hall. The two youngsters, triumphant in their match with the cabinet saunter down the hallway, moving straps in their hands. I hold up a finger.

'Ja, mein Herr?' the Smart One says.

'That scar,' I point to his arm.

He rubs a hand over the scar.

'Ja, I got it in the Congo...' he says. 'Excuse me, mein Herr.'

His excessive politeness was hammered into him by a drill instructor and 1st sergeant. This young man is a veteran of our war in the Congo. Immediately he has my sympathies.

I go back inside and lie down. A knock on the door awakens me. It is incessant to the point of obnoxiousness. Slowly I rise.

'Ja, ja!' I shout in my old trench voice, 'Please allow a body to wake up.'

'Oh, sorry!' replies a voice in English.

I put my clothes on and make my way toward the door and open it. Before me stands an American man. I know so right away. His tan slacks are clean and pressed. So is his blue button-down shirt. His black hair is perfectly combed to the side and feathered on his forehead. His face is chiseled, eyes bright and inquisitive. The American looks like he wants to sell me something.

'Hi!' he says in the way of over- enthusiastic Americans. 'My mover tells me they were making a lot of noise and woke you up.'

'Ja.'

'Well I am sorry for that.'

'Nein, nein,' I say. 'It is all right. You are moving in.'

'This is a bad way to get to know your new neighbors,' he says. The American extends his hand, 'I'm Bob Baker.'

We shake hands. 'A pleasure,' I say.

'My family and I just moved in down the hall.'

'Ja, I see.'

'So, we hope to see you around.'

'Ja, of course, as do I.'

Bob Baker looks over my shoulder and sees my studio.

'An artist?' He asks.

'I have been a painter all my life.'

'Oh, good,' Bob Baker says. 'My wife loves to paint and it will be wonderful for her to have someone to get on with.'

Yes, I think, *that is why I am here, to keep the company of bored American house fraus. Such American impudence.*

'Perhaps this evening you could come over for a coffee?'

I see in the man's eyes that he is desperate to meet someone. Americans need to be liked. I agree. Besides, his wife is an artist and it would be nice to meet a young painter, to have someone to talk to about the craft.

Finally I am allowed my nap.

A few hours later I rise, clean up and put on my best suit, black, with matching tie and white shirt. The suit is old and a bit ramshackle but it will do. When ready I walk down the hallway and politely knock on the door. Bob Baker answers. His face lights up in the American way and he invites me in.

'Honey!' he shouts.

Mrs. Baker comes out from the kitchen. She is tall like her husband with brown hair and eyes. Her facial features are soft and understated, restrained even. I would have assumed Mrs. Baker to be an Englishwoman were it not for the gleam in her eye, that American gleam of optimism and opportunity. They are remarkable that way.

I click my heels, bow and introduce myself.

'Charmed,' Mrs. Baker says.

I look around. Their apartment is the mirror of mine. The floors have a new sheen though and I can smell the fresh coat of paint. The Bakers have not yet been able to unpack their possessions and boxes are stacked along the walls and in the corner. I hear a tea kettle.

'Ah,' Mrs. Baker says. She heads to the kitchen. Over her back she says, 'I wasn't sure if you wanted tea or coffee so I am making both.'

'Please do not trouble yourself, Mrs. Baker.'

'It is no trouble,' she replies. 'And please call me Aggie'

'And we have a daughter,' Bob Baker says. 'She is at the embassy.'

'Embassy?' I ask.

'Oh, yes!' Bob Baker says, 'I almost forgot. I'm a staffer at the embassy.'

'Staffer?' I ask.

'Yes, I work for Ambassador Brundage, sort of an assistant.'

'Ah, I see.'

From the kitchen Aggie says, 'Would you care for coffee or tea?'

'Tea, please,' I reply.

'Won't you sit?' asks Bob Baker.

He motions for me to sit down. It is an American couch, white and made of synthetic leather. Across is a matching love seat and in the corner a white, angular desk made to match. All factory made without a hint of craftsman-ship. The pieces are new and modular. Americans, they have no taste.

Bob Baker sees me admiring the furniture and says, 'Oh, yes, the den set. I brought it from home.'

'Ah.'

'Actually, a present from my mom and dad,' he says. 'For graduating from the foreign service school.'

'Ah,' I say, 'So how long have you been with the American Foreign Ministry?'

'We call it the State Department,' Bob Baker corrected.

I blush. 'Of course.'

'This is my sixth year.'

'And before Deutschland?'

'After the foreign service school, the State Department posted me to Peking. I was a liaison with the Kuo Min Tang's political office.'

'Most interesting,' I say. 'Did you ever meet Chiang Kai Shek?'

Bob nods, 'On one or two formal occasions. Honestly, word at the embassy was he could be very difficult to deal with.'

'Do you speak Chinese?' I ask.

'The language is actually Mandarin.'

'Oh.'

'Very little I'm afraid,' Bob Baker says. 'But Aggie and I have been working on our German for a year now.'

I look over at Mrs. Baker. 'We are coming along,' she says.

'Ah good. May I hear some?'

I expected Mrs. Baker to blush, but instead she wished me a good evening and in badly accented but fluent German told me about learning German. I give a courteous nod and reply, 'Das is good, ja!'

'You should see Erica,' Mrs. Baker says. 'She has taken right to it.'

'Children, of course. They learn languages so quickly. I wish I had taken a language as a child.'

'You learned English later then?' Mrs. Baker asked.

'Yes, after the war, for my first trip to America.'

'You've been to the states?' Bob Baker asked.

'Ja, an artist's fellowship for veterans of the war.'

'You were in the war?'

'Ja, with the 16ᵗʰ Reserve Infantry Regiment. West and Eastern front. If you care to, sometime I can show you the sketches I made.'

'I didn't tell you, honey?' Bob Baker asks, 'He's an artist.'

Mrs. Baker's face comes alive. It was then that I saw her intelligence. At first I was inclined to think of Mrs. Baker as a pretty but vapid American house wife. But in her eyes, I see her inner light and curiosity.

'Ja, I have been an artist my entire life.'

'I love the arts,' she says, 'I paint myself. My materials are not unboxed yet.'

Bob Baker points his thumb at his wife. With love and admiration he says, 'She's good.'

Mrs. Baker blushes and swipes a hand at her husband. 'I am just a hobbyist,' she says. 'Not a professional artist like you.'

I sip my tea and say, 'I would like to see your work.'

'Sure!' she says with typical American enthusiasm.

I do not admit my selfish reasons for wanting to see Mrs. Baker's work. I am old and jaded. Often a young person, and I doubt if Frau Baker is past thirty, filled with youth and enthusiasm can invigorate someone such as myself.

'I was in the service myself,' Bob Baker says.

'Service?' I ask, not quite understanding the American meaning of the word.

'Oh!' Mrs. Baker intervenes. 'He means the military.'

'Oh yeah,' says Bob Baker. 'Army all the way!'

'Ah,' I sip my tea. 'The United States Army. Tell me, were you in the Philippine Conflict?'

'Yes.'

'Ah, so that is why your state department posted you to Manila.'

Bob Baker nodded.

'But just with a civil affairs unit. We dealt with civies, Moro chiefs and such. I've never been shot at.'

'I have,' I sip my tea again. 'An experience I would not like to relive...'

CHAPTER 4

1914

——

THE SUN HAD NOT YET come up when our train stopped at Alfenstels. We were in our boxcars all day and night. Some boxcars had the stench of horses, others of death as they had transported wounded. Indeed the boxcar in which my own 1ˢᵗ Company travelled still had blood stains on the floor boards. After a rough night we were glad to disembark even though we knew a long march lay ahead. In the dark our officers formed us into columns. Sgt. Ammon walked up and down the line shouting at and berating us. We assembled quickly if only to shut up Ammon. Within minutes the 16ᵗʰ Reserve Infantry Regiment was marching east, along with several other regiments combined to form the 6ᵗʰ Bavarian Reserve Division, then part of the 8ᵗʰ Army.

It would be weeks before we stopped marching.

Only in the daylight could we see the results of the great Battle of Tannenberg. The detritus of war was almost entirely Russian, a never-ending scene of smashed rifles, broken wagons, and bloated horses. We saw Russian cloaks seemingly wadded up and dropped, cloth caps caked in mud and blood, discarded rifles. This was the carpet left by a shattered army. It was not long until we saw prisoners. These Russians looked even worse off than their French counterparts in the west. On the side of the road they were gathered in large pens, each held thousands of men. They looked destitute in their rotting summer uniforms and I wondered how long till parties were sent out to collect all the cloaks and caps so causally thrown aside in August. We took one of our rest breaks on the side of the road by one of the camps. I was surprised to see the Russians cordoned off by razor wire with only a few guards and machine guns here and there. As we milled about I asked one of the guards about the lack of German troops.

'We need every last man at the front,' he said.

'What about them?' I pointed to the Russians.

'Them?' he asked. 'They do not want to fight. Most are glad to be away from the fighting. They killed their officers when they tried to stop them from surrendering.'

I nodded, 'Poor wretches.'

The guard scoffed. 'Do not feel bad for them.'

'They are still men.'

'You would not think so, had you seen what they did to German villages between here and the border.'

Now it was my turn to scoff. 'Oh, come now. Propaganda.'

'I saw it with my own eyes,' he scowled at the Russians. 'They should be shot.'

Later that day we saw Russian depravity for ourselves. We entered a small village, each house was systematically dismantled, furniture, floor boards and roof tiles stacked and burned. The fiends had also taken the time to desecrate the cemetery, paying particular attention to the Jewish section. Here they knocked over every gravestone and emptied every tomb. We saw this scene several more times as we marched east. Never again would I look at Russians the same way. To me they have ever since been fiends. Today when the young or naïve question the need for our anti-Russian alliance with the peoples of Eastern Europe and Das Vistula Korps, I remind them of what the Russians did in East Prussia 50 years ago.

With reinforcements pouring in from the west, Hindenburg resumed the offensive. Hindenburg's latest offensive around the Masurian lakes cracked the Russian line. The Czar's armies had no choice but to fall back. To our south Prittwitz and his army drove the Russians out of German territory and forced them back on Warsaw. This city, now the capital of the great Polish state, was the Russian military center on the frontier. Together with Tannenberg, these battles marked the beginning of the end of the Russians in Poland.

We in the 16th Reserve Infantry Regiment and the 6th Reserve Infantry Division experienced it only as a distant flash on the horizon, rising and falling with each second like a lightning storm only a thousand times more powerful, the yellow light bounced off the clouds and reflected back down to earth. Out of sync with the light extravaganza was a low, steady rumble like a hundred trains running north to south. These were the massed artillery pieces of the 8th Army, hammering away at the Russian beasts. I have been shot at and shelled, but nothing I have experienced has ever been as ominous and foreboding.

The deluge lasted through the night and into the morning. By noon the rumble felt more distant and by evening we knew it was indeed further away. We watched that night almost in disappointment. The great thunder flash on the horizon was now just distant pinpricks of light popping off in the distance and snapping like Chinese firecrackers. Most of us watching the far-off conflagration grew bored and fell asleep. Before dawn, Sgt. Ammon rousted us out of our sacks and mustered the 1st Company. Lt. Weisgerber walked up and down the line shouting, 'Come now you lazybones. The enemy is running! *Mach schnell!*'

And so we marched. During the whole of November I recall marching, only marching across the cold, wet Baltics. Always the sounds of war were on the horizon a constant, distant rumble of artillery fire, nothing like the sustained deluge before the battles around the Masurian Lakes, but impressive nonetheless. For weeks we marched toward the guns without actually getting closer to them. Oh, we saw the results of battle, we did. Here a field worked up by our guns, the soft, wet earth churned over with only a wagon wheel or smashed rifle butt showing the violence that had befallen the place. There we passed a village, if not shot up by our own troops then burned to the ground by retreating Russians. Often the villagers congregated in the pathetic remains of their homes wrapped in German blankets and eating German rations. Once when we stopped for dinner beside a village, I asked an old man why Russian troops would so brutalize their own people, he spat and yelled, 'We are not their people! We are Lithuanians!'

The man's face was withered, almost like an old piece of leather, his nose a crooked beak. I doubt if there was an ounce of fat on him. He was so old he probably grew up hearing stories from veterans of the great struggle against Napoleon. I apologized to the old man and asked if I could make a quick sketch of himself. Perhaps sensing that this was his chance at immortality he smiled and agreed. I made a quick sketch of the old man, harrowed and withered, but also strong. I gave him a look and asked him to sign it. He did so, 'Ivan Applebaum' I saw in surprise. He was a descendant from Teutonic settlers from the 16th century!

The regiment was deep into Lithuania and nearing Vilnius when we finally stopped marching. The front was close again, our guns constantly raged at the enemy. We watched from a distance one night as they hammered the city's defenses. In the morning we marched forward. By the time night fell again we were closer to the barrage than we had ever been before. The yellow and orange artillery bursts didn't just dominate the horizon, they were the horizon. They were just a few kilometers away now.

That morning for the first time in weeks we had hot food, coffee and tea. I was suspicious.

Over oatmeal I said to Schmidt, 'I guess this means we are going into line?'

'You think so?'

'Ja,' I replied. 'We have not had hot food in weeks. Why change now?'

Schmidt bit into a biscuit and nodded, 'Maybe, maybe not.'

Just then Lt. Weisgerber walked by.

'Aye! Lieutenant!' Schmidt called. He pointed a thumb to me. 'He thinks we're going into the fight.'

'He thinks right. Get ready.'

Schmidt swallowed hard, nearly choking on a big piece of biscuit.

Indeed when breakfast was finished, 1st Company assembled with the rest of the regiment and Colonel List came down to speak to us.

'Well, men,' he began. 'We have done little else but march all this month. Today that ends. Today we attack!'

Behind him Sergeant Ammon led us in a cheer and then Deutschland Über Alles. Colonel List moved on to 2nd Company and left it to Lt. Weisgerber to explain what we were doing.

'Men,' he said. 'The Russians have made a stand on this ground before Vilnius. Last night the 10th Division broke through just to our front. Our mission is to advance into the gap and widen it. There is a small village to the north and east. That is our target. We shall take it and hold it against counterattack. As we do so the 17th RIR will pass behind us and further widen the breach.'

We in the 1ˢᵗ Company looked at the lieutenant and then at each other.

'We can do it,' Schmidt said.

'Ja,' I replied.

The regiment advanced with my own 1ˢᵗ Company leading the way. We entered the battle area. Here was ground churned up by war, smashed trees and broken equipment and bodies. While our grave diggers had recovered the bodies of dead Germans, Russians still lay where they fell. Here a Russian lying face down in the mud, there a trio of Russians clumped around a machine-gun. In this way one could piece together the battle. I saw that our own men attacked and breached the Russian defenses, a shallow trench line with a few boughs and logs for camouflage. I chanced a look inside one of the trenches. A ghastly sight, it was filled with dead Russians all piled upon one another.

We marched until we could see the new front line. There were our men, two rows of German soldiers occupying a position before a stream bed. The bed rose a meter or so and was covered with vegetation. The troops there occasionally fired a round or two at the Russians to their front, whom we could not yet see. I saw Colonel List walk forward and consult with another officer. A minute later the troops on the river bed stood and trotted off to the left, leaving the way clear for us. Lt. Weisgerber ordered our company forward. We trotted to the stream bed and filed right. Behind us 2ⁿᵈ Company filed left. The 3ʳᵈ and 4ᵗʰ Companies occupied our former positions so that our battalion formed a box.

Lt. Weisgerber said, 'Two hundred meters to our front...' the tac-tac-tac sound of a machinegun interrupted him, 'Two hundred meters to our front is the village.'

A few meters down the line, one of my squad mates poked his head above the embankment to have a look. I heard a crack and a moment later his head split in two. The soldier fell back and rolled off the embankment. We all sat there shocked at the sudden death of the soldier we had known for months. Weisgerber seemed to hyperventilate. He took several deep breaths and ordered, 'Stay down!'

We all nodded. Someone said, 'Jawohl.'

'Our artillery will fire in...' he checked his watch, 'just under a minute. It will shell the village. Wait for the whistle, then we advance.'

Above us passed a cacophony of screaming shells that slammed into the village. I could not hear Schmidt as he tried to talk to me. I could not even hear myself think. So badly I wanted to see what our shells were doing to the village, but after the death I had just witnessed I didn't dare poke my head up. As the shelling continued, Lt. Weisgerber blew his whistle. We barely heard it. He waved his hands, getting our attention.

'Company advance!' he shouted.

Gingerly, we rose.

'Advance!'

We climbed the embankment and stepped right into the stream. I was up to my knees in cold, clear water. My teeth chattered, because of the cold or the enemy fire I have never known. We worked our way out of the stream. Here the Lieutenant ordered us to the ground. Before us was a collection of stone houses, perhaps a dozen in all, arrayed around a wooden church and spire topped with an onion dome and Orthodox cross. Most of the homes were damaged in the barrage but the church appeared unscathed. It would not long remain so. Just before the village I saw a line of churned up earth. This must be the Russian front line. Already men were moving about within. Colonel List saw it too and I heard him shout, 'First and Second Companies forward!'

Lt. Weisgerber blew his whistle and shouted, 'Go! Go! Mach schnell!'

The Russians on the other end of the field were still a bit stunned by our own barrage so we were able to jog forward several meters. The Russian deluge began and my life, my very being, changed forever. Still I can recall the tac-tac-tac of those Russian machineguns and the quick crack of their rifles. All around me men fell. I tripped and fell face first in the mud. Instinctively I got up, even as Russian bullets kicked up mud around me, splattering my face. I got to my feet and fell over a dead comrade. As I tried to hoist myself to my feet someone stepped on my arm and fell forward in front of me. He writhed on the ground in pain, but there was little I could do for him. I got up, rifle in hand and ran forward.

Bullets whipped past me and smacked into the wet earth or sickeningly, into my comrades. Everywhere I looked someone was falling forward or flying backwards. My face was wet, I could not tell whether with mud or blood of my comrades. I glimpsed Schmidt but quickly lost him as a line of Russian bullets kicked up a geyser of mud in my face. I ran forward, tripping over another comrade. I struggled to extricate my face from the mud. I could not move my legs and thought for certain I had been shot. I looked behind me and saw a dead comrade lying across the back of my knees. I freed one leg and rolled the dead man off me, then I got up and ran again. Now with several of my fellow Germans we stood at the lip of the Russian trench. My comrades and I raised our rifles and fired into the trench. The man to my right flew backwards, a bullet having slammed into his chest. I jumped down into the trench and landed on a dead Russian soldier. Had I shot him? Who knows? Other German soldiers were beside me. I pressed myself against the trench and looked north. I raised my rifle and fired at the Russians running away. I do not know if I hit anybody but I saw several men stumble forward. I kept firing until someone grabbed my shoulders. I turned around and realized it was Schmidt. His face was bloody, covered by a stream that ran down from a cut on his scalp and was already caking around his eyes. I set him against the trench wall and went back to work.

The Russians were hiding behind and within several of the stone houses and firing on us. I heard and felt their bullets zipping overhead. Their tac-tac-tac machinegun fire emanated from the church. Off in the distance I could hear a whistle. I glanced behind me and saw 3rd and 4th Companies advancing. Lt. Weisgerber blew his whistle. 'Up! Up!' he shouted. 'Mach schnell!'

No coward he, Lt. Weisgerber climbed on the lip of the trench and waved for us. I followed him, as did Schmidt and many others. We all ran forward several steps and fell to the earth. Here we fired on the Russian church, now perhaps fifty meters off. As I pumped round after round into the church I saw bits of wood and paint fleck off the boards, we shot the church full of bullet holes, but the gun within kept firing, tac-tac-tac. By now our massed rifles, those that were left of the 1st and 2nd companies, maintained a steady drone of fire at the church. Finally the Russian machinegun stopped. Lt. Weisgerber ordered us forward. I ran with all my might and slid into the wall of the church, a few meters to the right of the window from which the gun was firing. Someone took a hand grenade and threw it in the window. I closed my eyes against the wall-shaking blast.

Lt. Wesigerber blew his whistle again. 'Forward! Forward! Follow me!'

It was the lieutenant's cry of 'follow me' that got us off our feet.

We followed the lieutenant as he led us out of the village. Now we faced another field, brown and tan with winter grass. A few shell craters pocked the field. I saw one Russian body and beyond that, Russian troops running away.

'Here!' the Lieutenant shouted. 'Form a line!'

He arrayed the 1st Company in a line in front of the village.

'Here! Here!'

By then we heard the crack of Russian rifles and felt bullets whizzing past. Off to my left I heard the sickening wet smack of a bullet hitting someone.

'Dig!'

Weisgerber ducked, took his shovel off his belt and plunged it into the wet dirt. Behind him Schmidt and I drove our shovels into the earth. Fortunately the ground was not frozen and within minutes we dug ourselves a shallow fox-hole in which we could crouch. Behind us the 2nd Company occupied positions in the houses and church. Each window bristled with rifles. Men even lay flat on the roofs. While we were still digging, Russian artillery exploded to our front. Then another barrage came over. This one we could tell would land right on us.

The impacting shells tore at and rocked the earth around us. The blasts shook dirt off the lip of our foxholes and showered us with debris. Schmidt wet himself. I tried to scream but I had no air in my lungs. My stomach seemed to flip, my loins retracted in on themselves, my mouth went dry as the shells fell all around us. I cried out with each earth-shattering blast and felt only relief when the barrage lifted. Never have I known that kind of fear. Lt. Weisgerber blew his whistle and shouted, 'Here they come!'

I looked over the lip of our foxhole and indeed, several dozen Russian soldiers were coming out from behind the rock wall. The first line ran out several meters and then fell to the ground. They fired as the second line came out from behind the wall. These passed their comrades who got up and followed.

Lt. Weisgerber shouted, 'Fire! Fire!'

In an instant our entire line came alive with the crack and snap of Mauser rifles. Behind us our two company machineguns opened fire, tat-tat-tat, spitting bullets at the oncoming Russians. Each snap of the rifle penetrated my ear drums. To this day I feel a faint but constant ringing in my ears, always I am reminded about this awful day.

It is here that I saw the Russians up close. Driven on by their officers, the Russians came at us like wild animals. For not one second did I doubt their resolve. It was as if they were snarling beasts deep from the Russian steppes. But even these fiends could not stand up to the hail of fire we threw out at them. The Russians retreated and took cover behind the wall. They fired on us but hit nothing, something I noticed throughout the war. The Russian cannot shoot. But he can fire an artillery barrage. Once more the very ground about us shook with the rumble of the Russians' big guns. I cried out again, and as a shell landed near my foxhole, I actually cried. Schmidt broke down as well and we clung to one another sobbing, convinced that this was the last earthly contact we would know.

'Why can't you be a woman?!' Schmidt shouted.

The barrage moved on, leaving Schmidt and me on the floor of the foxhole.

A bugle blew, a rifle volley cracked out from the front and the Russians moved forward again. This time our own artillery caught the Russians in the open. They had no chance. One moment a line of savage Cossacks was advancing toward us; the next they were gone in a fog of artillery. When our own guns stopped firing, the Russians were back behind their wall. There they remained for the rest of the day and so we remained. Our own guns shelled the Russians. On Colonel List's orders, we took the opportunity to dig deeper. Furiously Schmidt and I piled the dirt high above the lip of the foxhole until it was nearly a trench.

At sundown the Russians came again. This time they advanced in small groups, one rushing forward several meters before falling to the churned up ground. Many gruesomely took cover behind the bodies of their fallen comrades. The lucky ones took shelter in one of the many shell craters that pocked the field. The Russians approached closer than they had ever had. Only our massed rifle fire stopped them. Many Russians retreated back to their own lines but many, perhaps dozens, were trapped in the no man's land. We gunned them down without mercy. Those who could do so retreated back to their positions, leaving dozens of dead and wounded behind.

As the sun went down we heard the wounded's moans and screams - pitiful cries for help from their comrades. Schmidt and I asked Weisgerber if we could take them water.

'Nein!' he replied angrily.

'But....' I protested.

'It could be a trap!' he explained. 'We have reports of the Russians luring German soldiers.'

'Oh.' I relented.

Later I came to doubt these reports.

Lt. Weisgerber ordered us to shoot any Russians trying to help their comrades trapped in no-man's-land. What followed was the most horrific night of my life. A night filled with the animal-like wailing of dying men; men crying for their comrades, men crying for their sweethearts or mothers, men reduced to dying animals in the cold mud. The crack of our rifles permeated the night but brought no relief. We killed men for no other reason than trying to help their friends.

Morning revealed of horror-scape and a white flag. A Russian officer came forward and spoke with Lt. Weisgerber. He gave the Russians fifteen minutes to evacuate their wounded. I suppose a few were alive. That truce was shattered when Weisgerber spotted a Russian carrying off several rifles. He ordered us to open fire. We killed that unlucky Russian and several others. I actually saw one man waving his arms frantically and shouting 'Nyet! Nyet!'

From then on we in the List Regiment knew we could expect no mercy from the Russians.

We remained in the village throughout the next day, facing off against an enemy who did little except return our stares. Other regiments marched past and behind us toward Vilnius and other points northeast. We remained awake the next night watching the flashing horizon and listening to a great battle unfold. As dawn came the flashes disappeared but the roar of the guns remained, though they grew more distant until they all but stopped in the afternoon. We did not know it yet, but the 8th Army had won a great battle, part of Hindenburg's drive on Vilnius.

In the List Regiment, rumor circulated that the Russian counterattack was going to fall on us. Indeed someone in high command believed those rumors because another regiment, I never did learn which one, took positions a half kilometer behind us in expectation that the Russians would attack us. That night a ferocious artillery barrage churned the ground all around, showering us with dirt, rocks, branches, whatever the earth would give. Once more Schmidt and I lay at the bottom of our trench clinging to one another like desperate lovers, grasping one another tighter with each blast. The barrage lasted fifteen minutes but no follow-on assault came. That morning the reserve regiment passed through our lines and attacked the Russians to our fore. But they found the Russians had abandoned the defensive line, most likely under cover of the previous night's barrage. The other regiment stood in the Russians' trenches, holding up souvenirs, abandoned rifles, hats, coats, even a broken machinegun.

'Ja, these shirkers will take those souvenirs home and claim they won them in heroic battle against the Russians.'

I spat.

Schmidt pointed to a soldier holding up a Russian pistol. 'I want a pistol.'

We remained in place all that day and the next. As we remained stationary, the fighting moved northwest till we could no longer hear the rifles and machineguns. After the third day, Colonel List visited our company and gave us a motivational talk, complimenting the men of the 1st Company on our conduct throughout. Then he told us we would be staying in this village for some time. There was much groaning and even a shout of 'Why can't we stay in Vilnius?'

Sgt. Ammon shouted for silence in the ranks. Then Colonel List said, 'You want to stay in Vilnius?'

Even I said, 'Ja.'

'There is no Vilnius!' List shouted.

We were stunned into silence.

'Those guns serenading us the last few days were shelling Russian forces in Vilnius. Now the Russians have withdrawn and the guns have moved on. All that is left is rubble. We are better off here.' List cleared his throat. 'I have been assured we shall be here through December. The 17th Regiment will occupy the ground to our left, the 18th to our right. We are part of the 6th Army's general reserve and shall protect the left, rear flank.'

We were resigned to our new role.

It was not interesting or glamorous work. To be frank, after the last few days we had had enough of that. Out of my 1st company, forty were dead and ninety three wounded. I knew that other companies had suffered similar casualties. We established our perimeter at the Russians' old trench line. It was easy enough. Over the course of the cold, wet days we deepened the trenches, piling earth high around each side. Under Lt. Weisgerber's direction we dug a communications trench leading back to the village. We spent much time shoring up the bullet-riddled homes against the winter.

We also established a firewood patrol, with each platoon contributing men for daily forays into the countryside. These were more than potentially dangerous, several times a week our patrols encountered Russian counter-patrols and fighting ensued. Fortunately we suffered no casualties. After the beating they took in and around Vilnius, the Russians had little stomach for sustained combat. Soon we in the Regiment developed a relationship with the locals, and they began warning us when Russian troops set out from their own lines. This intelligence was very fruitful. More often than not we were able to avoid Russian patrols and on a few occasions ambushed theirs.

We were bored but at least we were warm and dry. Over the weeks we made the small houses impenetrable to the Russian wind and rain. Each platoon made one house its own and kept at least two men there at all times, lest our stash of worldly loot be pilfered by another platoon. For my own platoon this included several chairs, a dozen Russian blankets and a few household odds and ends. I must say that I enjoyed the art etchings in our plundered porcelain Russian tea-pot, a series of birds and flowers interwoven with a wisteria vine. Some of the wood bowls and cups had carvings as well. In this home hung an idealized wood carving of Czar Nicholas. We used to throw pebbles at it. Doing so became a kind of game to see who could hit the czar's head. I was never much good but Schmidt nailed the czar every time.

As Christmas approached, thoughts of home increasingly turned to religion. Naturally, men of the 1st Company gravitated to the village's small church. This took heavy fire during our battle for the village but men invested considerable effort into repairing the church. When these repairs were completed our more religious members convened a daily mass there within, which I thought strange since this church was consecrated in the Russian Orthodox faith. It all seemed rather silly to me - the mixture of two faiths in this way. I never had much use for religion at all so I wasn't very interested.

One morning the firewood patrol came back with an evergreen. With Lt. Weisgerber's permission they set up the tree outside the church. From there my comrades spent much of their free time making decorations for the tree and by the morning of Christmas Eve the tree had garlands and carved wood ornaments and a star made from a glass pitcher someone found within the church. I did not participate. Knowing my own artistic inclinations, Lt. Weisgerber asked me to sketch the tree. Seeing no harm in doing so, I made said sketch. I did another sketch of that night's ceremonies.

I loathe religion in all forms but there is no denying the intrinsic aesthetic beauty of 1st Company's Christmas Eve service. Dutifully I sketched and later added color. The men all gathered before the tree. Several lit candles hung from the tree and one could see a faint glow coming from the church door, a dim but strong yellow blotch of light. Whether it is the result of fire or something else, I leave to the viewer. The men hold hands and sing carols. The far, far horizon glows with the yellow light of artillery. I embellished this of course but felt it added to the sense of the moment.

We were weary by the new year, which marked six months for us all away from our families. January certainly began bleakly and we all wondered if we would ever leave that dismal, dreary village. Though a change in the weather was still months away, hope did spring. For on January fifth we heard of Hindenburg's great victory at Minsk. Here he destroyed two entire Russian armies, inflicting a hundred thousand casualties and taking another hundred thousand prisoners. A few days later we saw the fruits of Hindenburg's victory as a never-ending stream of Russian prisoners marched down the road past our village.

Watching those wretched Russians march past, I knew we had won the war. I expressed this sentiment to Schmidt.

'Come now,' he replied as we covered our noses against the stench of these Russian beggars. 'How can you tell all that just from seeing these men? Why, I bet the *poilus* in Napoleon's army thought the same thing in 1812.'

'Just look at them. Their uniforms are in tatters. And smell them.' I made a point of inhaling deeply. 'This is a defeated army. They seem more like Napoleon's *poilus* retreating from Moscow than ravaging Russian Cossacks.'

Lt. Weisgerber walked up behind us. 'He has a point Schmidt.' He said. 'And look at how few of us are needed to guard that mass of men.'

Indeed I would have said that the ratio was perhaps one guard for every twenty prisoners. Those Russians could have overwhelmed their captors at any time. They simply did not have the will to do so.

Events proved me right.

Hindenburg followed up his victory at Minsk by crushing another Russian army at Vitsyebsk. This victory secured both Minsk and Vilnius. More importantly, Hindenburg destroyed the last Russian army in the west. Sensing that the tide was inexorably with us, Romania declared war and sent two whole armies into Ukraine at once threatening Sevastopol and Kiev and securing our strategic southern flank.

Hindenburg could have marched on Smolensk or even Moscow and St. Petersburg had he chosen to do so. It all seemed to happen so fast, but in truth merely ten days passed between Hindenburg's victory at Minsk and Romania's declaration of war. Five days after that, word circulated through camp that the Russian Czar had abdicated. None of us were quite sure what that meant. But the peasants around us did. Upon learning of the Czar's abdication, and the personal assurances from Colonel List that it was true, the Lithuanians broke out in celebration and invited us to partake. So as to prevent fraternization, Colonel List confined us to quarters. Here we passed the night in great debate over what happened next.

I myself was as surprised as anyone by events. Instead of a regency, the reins of state were taken over by one of the Czar's ministers, Igor Kerensky. No fool was he. Though some in Russia wanted to continue fighting, Kerensky understood that Russia had already lost the war. Through the Americans he began armistice negotiations.

In the February cold we waited. After morning formation and drill we would conduct patrols. On occasion we saw Russian patrols. A few scattered shots by each side was enough to drive the other away. After a time we had an unspoken agreement with the Russians on that matter - each would fire a few rounds and withdraw. Lt. Weisgerber ordered us to aggressively pursue the Russians, but he was just passing orders on from Captain Von Zech, who no doubt received the same from Colonel List. Nobody's heart was in it, and nobody wanted to die in a war that was soon to end. This is how we occupied our mornings. The afternoons and evenings were our own after guard duty.

I passed the time with my copy of Schopenhauer and by sketching various aspects of our village life. I must say, sketches of German soldiers chopping wood, or gathered around the camp fire or standing in line for dinner do not make for an exciting subject. But they accurately portray those cold months.

On March 1ˢᵗ Colonel List called the entire regiment to assemble at the field behind the village. As Schmidt and I gave ourselves a quick cloth bath in cold water he said, 'Do you hear that?'

'Do I hear what…?' Just then I picked up the fading echo of guns.

'They stopped.'

From another direction another battery of guns boomed but then faded too.

'It is not sustained enough to be a barrage,' said I. 'What on earth?'

'Perhaps just registering the guns?'

Sgt. Ammon stuck his head into our hut. 'Come now, you men, we shall not keep the Colonel waiting.'

Clad in gray coats and boots which crunched the snow beneath them, we stood at attention as Colonel List stepped onto a ragged Russian stool. He looked like the rest of us, and I admired him for this. His greatcoat was ripped in a few places, his boots, though expensive were scuffed. Upon his face the colonel wore a great bushy beard to protect against the winter. Even beneath the beard one could tell his face was more gaunt than when the war began. He shared our hardships and hibernated in ramshackle huts like the rest of us.

Sgt. Ammon called the regiment to attention.

Colonel List said, 'Men, you no doubt have heard guns off in the distance. Those are German guns and they celebrate.'

Schmidt and I looked at one another.

'Men, I tell you now, Kerensky has agreed to terms. As of midnight last night the war is over!'

We all threw our caps in the air and cheered joyfully. Schmidt and I grabbed one another and jumped up and down in unison. 'Do you hear?' he shouted. 'Do you hear!'

Sgt. Ammon roared, 'Silence! Silence in the ranks!'

Colonel List held out his hand. Before he said anything else, Sgt. Ammon shouted, 'Three cheers for Colonel List!'

We were overwhelmed with joy and no regiment cheered their commander with more gusto on that day for sure. The Colonel held up both hands for quiet and said, 'Now, three cheers for the men of the 16th Bavarian Reserve Infantry Regiment!'

Led by our commander, how we cheered again…

CHAPTER 5

1964

———

DER SPIEGEL'S MORNING HEADLINE IS interesting and amusing. French Navy Departs Oran blazes across the front page in ten centimeter type. By doing so, the editors report an important fact, but also mock the French. They certainly deserve it. In a sad response to our own Victory Week, the government of Charles de Gaulle has sent the French navy on a grand tour of the world. The *Der Spiegel* article includes a photograph of the impressive-looking French aircraft carrier *Bonaparte*. Behind her the battleship *Guizot* lies at anchor. The *Jean Bart*, billed as a state of the art cruiser, rounds out the contingent of capital ships. Along with destroyer and frigate escorts, the flotilla numbers thirteen vessels. It is telling that in their choice of warship names, the French must harken back to their 19th century glory years. There are some panicky sorts in the Reichstag, Conservatives mostly, who worry that the French will use the occasion of this national holiday to launch a surprise attack upon the Reich. This is unlikely in the extreme. Without allies, France cannot possibly stand against us.

Though our two nations are at peace, France and Germany have a complicated relationship. France has never really come to grips with its defeat in 1914, forty years after Bismarck humiliated her in 1871. After the 1914 victory, Bethmann-Hollweg went out of his way not to humiliate France. We took a sliver of territory, the valuable Longwy-Brier iron basin, but in losing Congo to the Reich, Belgium suffered much more. Ever since the Treaty of Strasbourg, the French have plotted a war of revenge. They plotted such a war after 1871 and all that brought them was humiliating defeat. It seems the French have learned nothing.

In their quest for a new war, the French have few friends. Russia maintains a powerful army on our frontier but as of now Moscow is concerned with keeping its rebellious southern provinces loyal. Britain's interests do not in any way clash with Germany's, and after the folly of the last general European war, successive British Prime Ministers have avoided becoming too involved with the troublemaking French. In part to placate the French when Britain carved up the Ottoman empire, they took Palestine for themselves but gave France the old province of Syria. Thankfully Bethmann-Hollweg convinced the Kaiser to stay out of that region. In my view nothing good can come of European involvement in the Middle East. While Britain is having trouble with Zionist fanatics in Palestine, France is dealing with Christian separatists on the coast and violent revolutionaries in Algeria.

Many believe the French government foments these conflicts to keep the public distracted from trouble at home. And indeed the nation is deeply divided, much more so than Germany. Young and old, imperialists and self-determinationists. Those of the establishment that want to remain at odds with Germany, and the youth who want to move on after 50 years. Who can blame the young? They have no memory of the old France. They know only the new France, blocked by Germany, ignored by Britain and mocked by the United States. As the youth in Germany have a share in the new world of trade and exchange so, too, would the youth of France.

It seems that since 1914, France has shrunk. Her horizons extend barely beyond the Rhine and Pyrenees to the neglect of all else, including their empire. No wonder they face revolt in the Mediterranean. During the Pacific War Japan easily took French possessions in Southeast Asia and when the war was over, the United States had zero interest in returning these to France, despite Paris' vehement demands that they do so. Normally I think the non-Europeans of the world would do better to accept the steadying hand of the white man, but the Kingdom of Siam seems better off without the French.

The nation practices a kind of hyper-nationalism where all things in France must be French. They wage a Kulturekampf against the Swiss and Italian people within *L'isle de France*, insisting they speak only French and even going so far as to ban the Romanche and Italian languages in public and in schools. Those same schools emphasize French culture to the exclusion of all else. A

French art student will learn little of the works of Michelangelo or Leonardo, a young officer at St. Cyr will study only the campaigns of Napoleon, Martel, Conde and Turenne. French literature students are almost entirely ignorant of the great works by English and German authors.

The war does not stop at culture. In France they now have a saying, 'All things for France, all things from France'. The French government places heavy import taxes on dozens of goods, especially wine. Tariffs on wine imported to France approach 100%. In 1960, French wine manufacturers staged a 'wine party' inspired by the Americans' tea-party in which French thugs and bully boys stormed a freighter in Niece and dumped thousands of bottles of Italian wine into the bay. In Brest, French farmers blocked off the port because a freighter carrying a shipment of English beef lay at anchor. The blockade remained in effect until the beef went bad. A few years ago the de Gaulle regime passed a law banning the sale of any but French cars and mandating foreign cars off the streets by 1970- as if a Peugeot or Renault can pass muster against the craftsmanship and drivability of a German Mercedes, a BMW or an Audi.

While these cars represent the cutting edge in German automobile engineering, I find myself more amazed by the sheer utility of a Volkswagen. The latter was one of Speer's ideas, when he was minister of production in the 1940s. Speer's concept was brilliant in its simplicity - a streamlined, simple and efficient car, high quality of course, that any German worker can purchase.

I read further through the newspaper article on the French Navy, 'Chancellor Speer called the French Navy's so called 'grand tour' an unnecessary provocation. When asked if he planned to sortie the Kriegsmarine in kind, the Chancellor said they had no plans to do so at this time...' *Ahhh, smart,* I think. Why do anything provocative on the eve of our celebrations? I have always liked Chancellor Speer and even voted for him in the last election. He is an architect by trade and first gained public notice managing the Reich's Office of Construction during the Great Depression. The Kaiser liked him as did the Chancellor, and by the 40's Speer was a rising star in the old Bismarckian Conservative Party. Speer's hand is steady and his judgement wise.

At home, Chancellor Speer favors the cooperation of business and government to improve Germany. He has spent much of his first few years in office rebuilding and modernizing Berlin. Speer's government has constructed a great radial beltway around Berlin with several exits taking motorists to various points within the city. The beltway also links to the great Autobahn, the construction of which Speer oversaw during the Depression. On the colonies, Speer's is a sound policy of gradualism, training and developing the indigenous peoples till they are ready for self-rule. There are those in the world, mostly Americans, who believe in immediate independence. But I have been to Congo and have seen first-hand what happens when the untrained Negro is left to his own devices. I agree with the Chancellor - we should wait. Speer thinks the colonies might be ready for independence, or at least some kind of dominion status based on the successful British model, by the end of the century.

In foreign affairs Chancellor Speer is cautious and maintains a strong alliance against Russia. Today Poland and Romania are our closest allies. Those two small, brave nations fear Russia with good reason. Both nations maintain strong military establishments. The Poles for instance have a standing army of 200,000 men organized into two army groups and fourteen divisions. In 30 days, the great Polish nation can mobilize an additional one million men. These are augmented by our own Vistula Korps, an army of 70,000 men in five divisions deployed east of Warsaw. The Luftwaffe supports Das Vistula Korps out of the great airbase northeast of Wroclaw. The combined German-Polish force anchors the alliance's great left flank, as the General Staff calls it.

The Great Right Flank is anchored by Hungary in the north and Romania in the south. We have not deployed any troops to Romania. One look at the map explains why. The coastal plain is all but indefensible. The Romanian Army will defend Bucharest, but for the most part Romanian plans center on withdrawal to the great Carpathian redoubt in the northwest and wait for help to arrive from Germany. Hungary's Army of Carpathia anchors the northern end of the redoubt. Here an elite force of ten mountain brigades stands the eastern watch in the district of Muchacheve wisely seized by the new Hungarian government during Russia's troubles after the Great War. This force is augmented by the German 90th Light Division.

The Eastern Alliance's grand strategy is one of pin and hold. Polish, Romanian and Hungarian forces will absorb the initial Russian onslaught, pin them in place, and hold until reinforcements arrive from Germany. The

General Staff has some very interesting ideas in this regard and has organized what they call 'combined arms' corps. Here brigades of Panzers will advance in mass against Russian troops, pierce their line and tear up their echelon areas. *Panzerkrieg* they call it. The idea is indeed interesting but all theoretical. The General Staff has never had a chance to test their *Panzerkrieg*.

Even fifty years after the Great War the General Staff still worries about being caught in a two front war. But this seems unlikely to me. Such an effort would fall to France this time without the help of the English. Chancellor Speer maintains good relations with the British Empire. We will never be close friends, but there is no reason for our two empires to fight as we did during the Great War. Besides, Britain has as much interest in containing Russia as we do, what with India's vulnerable northwest frontier. Regarding America, well, in the 19th century Bismarck said that god watches over fools, drunkards and the United States. This is certainly the case today. Our relations with the Americans are distant but cordial. Since the Great Pacific War, America has been largely indifferent to events in Europe, preferring to leave Continental matters to their English cousins.

Herr Weder comes to my table.

He points to the paper, 'Can you believe those French?'

I purse my lips, 'Not surprising really.'

'They may try something,' Weder says. 'Like the Japanese did with the Americans.'

'Oh I doubt that,' I say. I hold up the map provided by *Der Spiegel*, 'See, the French fleet is sailing west not east. For the Mediterranean. And it says here that the French fleet intends to pass through Suez. The paper even says that the English may not allow them to do so.'

'It could be a trick.'

I laugh.

Herr Weder continues, 'Seriously. The British tell the French fleet they cannot pass through Suez and then they come back west and BAM!' He slaps his fist into his open palm, 'They take our fleet by surprise.'

'I really think this is unlikely.'

I snap my paper, hoping that Herr Weder will accept the hint. He doesn't, but Frau Weder does and calls her husband away.

CHAPTER 6
1915

———

THE 16TH RESERVE INFANTRY REGIMENT returned to Germany with great fan-fare. Huge crowds greeted us at every town. People cheered, children called after us for souvenirs and asked how many Russians we had killed. Young frauleins practically offered themselves to the men of the regiment. As we made the trek west, we wondered when we would return to Bavaria. But alas, some time would pass before the army discharged us. Instead we disembarked outside Berlin. Our regiment and the entire 6th Bavarian Division camped in a large field outside the city. It was our home for nearly a month. It seems that Bethmann-Hollweg planned a great parade to commemorate our victory. When King Ludwig learned of the celebration he demanded that Bavarian troops take a place of honor in the march. He also suggested the 6th Division as he liked the idea of a reserve division having proven its worth in the war.

This was not an unhappy time. The weather was turning in our favor and though we were under camp discipline, we were free to travel to Berlin and did so every weekend. It was a city ebullient with victory but also relief. As we walked the streets of Berlin and drank in the bars we heard much talk about the future. By then England launched its grand offensive against the Ottoman Empire. British Troops Drive on Baghdad!, proclaimed one head-line. Jerusalem Falls! read another. The more bellicose papers demanded the Kaiser act to save the Turks. Sitting at a café one afternoon with Schmidt, I read with amusement one editorial declaring, 'Having defeated France in the West, and the Russians in the East, will the Kaiser and Bethmann-Hollweg allow the English to threaten our southern flank?'

'Schmidt,' I said holding the paper for him to see, 'Look at this paper.'

Schmidt leaned forward and read. 'Fools!'

'I wager whoever wrote this piece never heard the sound of a bullet over his head.'

Schmidt sipped his beer and said, 'Nein. The war is very comfortable in Berlin.'

This paper had grandiose plans for the Kriegsmarine High Seas fleet to sail into the Mediterranean to save the Turks. But Admiral Hipper was dead set against such a move, as was Moltke. The Kaiser was content with what he had won. There was much to do besides.

Armchair diplomats planned the future settlement in the east. With the fledgling Kerensky government dealing with several rebellions in the west and south, and England waging war on the Ottomans, Germany more or less had a free hand. As I was Austrian, my comrades in the 1st Company assumed I was an expert in all things Habsburg and would be able to explain the goings on within the Hofburg.

The evening before the Grand Victory Parade my comrades and I stayed around the camp fire speculating about what Austria and Germany would demand from Russia.

'What do you think Austria wants in the east?' Schmidt asked me.

I shrugged and insisted I really could not say.

'Come now. You lived in Vienna. What will the new emperor want?'

Poor old Franz Joseph would die before the end of the year. Little did we know his empire would soon die as well.

Someone said, 'Did you see the paper this morning? Right now the Austrian Army is dismembering Serbia.'

'Can you blame them?' asked Schmidt. 'After they assassinated the Archduke. What would we do if Russia assassinated the Kaiser?'

'I suppose they will incorporate Serbia into the Empire.'

'Incorporate what?'

'Ja. They have reduced Belgrade to rubble,' Schmidt said. 'They have overrun most of the rest of the country.'

At that moment the Austrian Empire seemed strong and could take what it wanted. How wrong I was!

Our talk moved on to plans for home. Of course I really had no home to talk of. During the last few years, the 16ᵗʰ RIR was my home and for the first time I wondered what I would do when we were finally discharged. In truth I wondered if I should remain in the army for my own good.

Toward midnight Sgt. Ammon walked the tent line clapping his hands and shouting. 'Alright, that's enough. Fires out! Everyone douse those fires and get to sleep.' He came to our fire and kicked it. 'You bunch get some rest. We have a big day tomorrow.'

Grumbling we all stood up and made for our tents.

'If anyone of you falls out of formation tomorrow because you are hungover I'll have your hide!' Ammon shouted. 'Off with you now.'

The next morning dawned bright and clear. The 16th Reserve Infantry Regiment assembled on our makeshift parade ground. During the rush to war there had never been time to issue us formal dress uniforms, so we wore our field uniforms. At least these were cleaned and pressed. Sgt. Ammon personally inspected each and every one of us. Our uniforms and rifles were clean, buttons and boots shined, caps properly worn. After looking over the 1ˢᵗ Company, Sgt. Ammon put his hands on his hips, chewed his lower lip and declared, 'Well, you are no Prussian Guards but I suppose you will do.'

And so we marched. Before our regiment, Colonel List rode on a great black horse flanked by two riders, one carrying our regimental guidon, the other the blue and white checkered Bavarian flag. The 16ᵗʰ Reserve Infantry Regiment led the 6ᵗʰ Bavarian Division at the end of the Grand Review. The choice spots went to elite Wehrmacht units like the Prussian Guards. Berliners cheered us all the same. Young ladies threw flowers and garlands at our feet and children marched alongside us until we reached the great review stand before the Brandenburg Gate. Here sat the Kaiser. Around him were the general staff, Moltke, who had a victory to match that of his uncle in 1871, and the now immortal Hindenburg. A few rows back from the Kaiser sat King Ludwig. Our bearers dipped their flags in tribute, we presented eyes right, and Colonel List saluted.

Once past the reviewing stand, our part in the celebration was over. We milled about for an hour until trucks arrived to take us back to our encampment. To our surprise we were greeted by row after row of tables upon which lay a sumptuous feast. As we beheld the spread before us, Sgt. Ammon said, 'Well you beggars, Colonel List and Captain Von Zech arranged this little banquet, even though you lot do not deserve it. Enjoy!'

We each took a spot at the table. Sgt. Ammon called the regiment to attention and shouted, 'Three cheers for Colonel List!'

We cheered and then Sgt. Ammon shouted, 'Three Cheers for Captain Von Zech!'

We cheered once more.

Colonel List came forward and said. 'Let us now remember our comrades fallen in the great war in the east.' He looked over to our regimental chaplain. 'Father...' He came forward bowed his head and said the Lord's Prayer. He concluded, 'Oh Lord, we beseech thee to guide our Kaiser and our Reich in the tumultuous days ahead. Give him a steady hand and clear heart...amen.'

The Lord did just that.

Our own table had roast beef and pork and pitcher after pitcher of beer. My squad mates dug into the meal with great abandon. I indulged in the delicacies as well, even allowing myself a glass of beer. Throughout the afternoon the men made great tributes to Colonel List and Captain Von Zech. We were subjected to many a drunken tribute. We ate and drank and sang with great abandon until we exhausted the supply of food and beer. Many men organized parties to head back into Berlin and continue their revelry. Most of my squad went, but I did not. I had overeaten and was tired from the glass of beer; a lesson about alcohol I have never forgotten. I stayed in camp and sketched the grand parade. I have always been glad I did so, for these sketches became paintings and in the demand for material extolling our victory, those paintings became the first major works I sold after the war.

Throughout the night and early morning, sun-up for some, the regiment filtered back into camp. There was no reveille that morning and I was practically the only man in the regiment awake before noon. Which was just as well, as most of us could not have come to assembly if ordered to do so.

From then on we just waited with one question on all of our minds, when do we receive our discharges? Fortunately we had not long to wait. The

General Staff did not want excess troops lolling about Berlin with nothing to do, and with King Ludwig pressing Bethmann-Hollweg to release Bavarians from German command, three days after the Grand Review we boarded trains for Bavaria.

We arrived in Munich with great fanfare. It seems King Ludwig was impressed by the Kaiser's Grand Review and ordered his own ministry to put together an event of similar pageantry. Crowds greeted us and once more we marched, this time through the streets of Munich to the central square at Marienplatz. Once more we passed in review and saluted the king. In truth, by then all we wanted was to go home. But our ordeal was not yet over. Before the reviewing stand, the entire 6th Bavarian Division assembled and King Ludwig made a grand speech to us. In truth I remember not one of his words. All I recall is the constant grumbling among the men about standing in ranks as Ludwig went on and on. Even Colonel List seemed annoyed. Sgt. Ammon walked the ranks and in his sternest quiet voice called for silence. When the king blessedly finished, Colonel List dismissed us and we boarded trains once more, this time for our old Lechfeld barracks outside the city.

And so we came full circle and we waited for our discharges. Once more I wondered what I would do.

We remained in barracks for another few days.

One morning Sgt. Ammon called the entire regiment to parade ground assembly. Colonel List came before us and read a proclamation from King Ludwig.

'Be it known that by order of King Ludwig III the enlisted men of the 16th Reserve Infantry Regiment are hereby discharged...'

Colonel List could not finish reading as the cheers of the regiment drowned him out. Even Sgt. Ammon was unable to call the ranks to silence. Colonel List simply pocketed the proclamation and smiled.

We spent the rest of the day gathering our things. We turned in our rifles but kept our uniforms. I signed one document acknowledging the terms and length of my military service and another acknowledging my receipt of a small bonus of 100 marks. Lastly, I signed my discharge papers.

My time in the 16th Reserve Infantry Regiment was over.

So it was time for the men of the 16th Reserve Infantry Regiment to say goodbye. My comrades and I exchanged postal addresses. I had none to give.

On Schmidt's suggestion I went with him to Munich. He offered to let me stay with him. Having no wish to impose, I politely declined. I stayed in a flop house for a few days and looked for an apartment. Rental prices had fallen and with my pocket flush with 100 marks I had several options. I settled into a small apartment, not far from Munich's Inner City. There was not much to it, just a room, a kitchen and bath, the latter being something of a luxury. In truth, I did not need much.

Once I was settled, my books unpacked, my studio set up, I went to work. The next few months were strange.

Given our victory, the public had an insatiable demand for material related to same. Sometimes the artist must yield to popular taste, at least if he wants to eat. So I painted scenes of glorious victory in east and west. I quickly sold my first such piece, *Germans on the Loire*, to the wife of a Munich doctor. Thereafter I did well for myself, usually moving a piece or two a week, more than enough pay my rent and provide for myself. I needed little. Simple food and little drink. I still had no use for tobacco. I was productive and providing for myself. It felt good to get back to art.

At night after I completed my work, I found myself pacing through my apartment as if I was looking for something I lost. I'd wander the streets sometimes hoping the people and company would fill the void within. More often than not I left these places feeling alone. At bedtime I tried to find comfort in my old friends, Schopenhauer and Karl May. The comfort found therein was fleeting and frankly, I found that I was not enjoying these things the way I once had. I delved deeper into Schopenhauer's ideas, reading the works that inspired him, Hegel, Nietzsche, Kant, but these works seemed like stand-alone ingredients, not a meal. For me, Schopenhauer had always been that meal but now he was unsatisfying.

I searched for other works. In Marx, I looked for meaning but found none. Marx identified the problems of the industrialized age but completely misdiagnosed their solution. As our own government would later show, the solution to poverty was government cooperation with business and industry, not their dissolution. I turned to the English. Their Burke made some good points but I have always admired the force of will the revolutionaries brought to France and especially Napoleon. After all, the Corsican transformed the country in his image.

I looked to newspapers. It was a pleasant enough exercise and I found I enjoyed being informed nearly up to the minute. Of course great events were transpiring here in Germany and Europe. With the collapse of the Russian army and the abdication of Czar Nicholas, Kerensky was left to clean up the mess. Almost immediately he faced a violent revolution led by adherents of Karl Marx. The ensuing civil war was short and sharp, after which Kerensky stood triumphant. This V.I. Lenin fellow was hung in Moscow's Lefortovo Prison. The victory gave Kerensky the gravitas he needed to consolidate his hold on power and put down rebellions in the Baltics and Ukraine.

I cannot say how much the Kaiser's government had to do with these insurrections, but it makes sense if the Kaiser and Bethmann-Hollweg aided them. As the Kerensky government was fighting for its life, Bethmann-Hollweg made his name redrawing the map of Eastern Europe. The actual task took more than a decade but by the time I was restlessly reading the papers, Bethmann-Holweg had already founded the Polish Republic and twisted the Austrians' arm to cede Transylvania to Romania. To this day those two grateful nations are our greatest allies in Europe while Vienna still seethes with resentment at the loss of their empire and eventual absorption into the German Reich.

While the mighty German army was bringing the Czar to heel, the English sought to redeem their national honor against the Turks. The English were clever and in retrospect I am glad that after the desultory fighting in Belgium and France in 1914, we settled our differences with the British Empire. That empire served the English well. A Commonwealth Army massed in Egypt and struck Palestine while an Anglo-Indian army landed in Basra and advanced up the Tigris-Euphrates River valley toward Baghdad. By the middle of 1915, the English were in Jerusalem and outside of both Damascus and Baghdad. They had made great progress but the tired Port marshalled its resources and held firm at these two crucial cities

The English acted so as to astonish the world. Under the leadership of their great Lord of the Admiralty, the Royal Navy sailed into the Dardanelles, the massive guns of their great battleships reduced the Turkish fortresses there to rubble. The Royal Navy then daringly landed troops at Gallipoli. Once the Royal Navy burst into the Bosporus, with several English divisions advancing along the shore, the Turkish army and state collapsed. For the first time in 500 years, Constantinople had Christian rulers.

Great consternation permeated the foreign ministry in Berlin and it is said that the Kaiser demanded the Bundeswehr and Kreigsmarine draw up plans to intervene on the Turks' behalf, lest his great Berlin to Baghdad railway never come to fruition. But Bethmann-Hollweg had no desire to launch another war when the one with Russia remained to be won. The Chancellor stood his ground and with time the Kaiser relented. In 1917 an understanding was reached between the German Reich and the British Empire. I am proud to say the Kaiser commissioned my friend Hugo Vogel to commemorate the treaty of Rome, hammered out by Bethmann-Hollweg and the great Winston Churchill. A print of the painting occupies an honored spot in my apartment.

Here one sees the two men before a map of Europe and the near east. Churchill sits, legs crossed, contemplatively chomping on a cigar while Bethmann-Hollweg stands opposite, pointing to an unseen place on the map, cigarette held between ring and middle fingers. Vogel has invited us to contemplate this moment when the two great men, representative of the world's two great empires made peace and made the world as we know it in 1964. The nation made by Kemal Ataturk buffers the Russian bear who struggles to keep the Caucasus region within its control and went to war within Persia over that nation's aid to Kazakh separatists. Palestine exists as a protectorate of the British Empire and sees a steady stream of Jews emigrating from Russia, much to the dismay of the English who would rather curry favor with the Arab majority.

Reading of these events only took up an hour or so of my day. And while interesting the newspaper could not fill the void I felt in my life.

All in all, I have to say that the years after our victory were the most difficult of my life.

One summer morning inn 1920, I received a letter which was unusual for me in those days as I corresponded with few. It was from a man named Hermann Struck, someone I had not met though I knew the name, vaguely. He had something to do with the arts community, I knew. Intrigued I opened and read:

Mein Herr,

Allow please an introduction. My name is Hermann Struck. I served with the wehrmacht during the late war. I tell you because it was during our demobilization that I met Lt. Franz Weisgerber, your company commander. On a long train ride through Germany we struck up a conversation. As we moved from the war and military life, I revealed that I am a professional etcher and had taught the craft at various universities. I have published a textbook on the matter titled, 'The Art of Etching'. It is with pride that I told Lt. Weisgerber that I made many etchings of our great Kaiser. In passing, Lt. Weisgerber mentioned that there was another artist in his regiment. We moved on, of course, but what he said always stuck with me.

Recently I have been active with a colloquium of veteran artists. We have been searching for veterans of the late war and I recalled Lt. Weisgerber's mentioning yourself. I wrote Herr Weisgerber and he provided me with your name and last known address. I hope this letter finds you well.

The purpose of this letter is to invite you to join the Great War Veterans' Artist Colloquium cruise to the United States in ten days' time. If you are interested please write back to me at…

I wrote back declaring my interest and I took the liberty of enclosing a few sketches I made during the march through Lithuania. A few days later I heard back from Herr Struck, he implored me to attend the cruise. The same day I wrote back saying I would indeed do so.

I took the train from Munich which ran west and then eventually linked into the main railway paralleling the Rhine. I had not been in this region since my old 16th RIR made the trek. For the first time since the war, I felt a bit of nostalgia. Of course the war did not touch the Rhineland at all. Still, there seemed a chasm between the Rhineland I saw in 1914 and 1920. The trek was dotted with the same towns and farms, but these had none of the kinetic energy present in 1914. I suppose they would not after two years of war. The stations were no more crowded than usual. One saw few soldiers as opposed to 1914 when we filled up the stations, fields, rest houses. I asked the old conductor if this is how the Rhine Valley normally looked. He explained, 'Ja, but France's trade has tamped down considerably the local economy.'

Indeed, since our victory over France the nation teetered on the brink of civil war, unable to stomach a pair of humiliating defeats within living memory. At this time France was under the control of a 'provisional' military dictatorship led by a general named Pétain who was one of the few French generals not to have the stench of defeat on his person. He had had nothing to do with the disastrous campaign of autumn 1914 and had even rallied French forces on the west bank of the Loire where they had held firm against a few minor pushes by our own army. In 1920 Pétain's 'provisional' dictatorship was in its 6th year. It would go on for another decade. Some call Pétain 'The French Cromwell'. Indeed he stabilized the nation, reformed the French army and fought several successful campaigns to hold on to what remained of the French overseas empire. Still, when he was shown the door by the fledgling chamber of deputies, most were glad to see him go. He lived for another 20 years, long enough to see France embroiled in still more colonial wars, all of which they lost. His partisans argue colonies were lost because Pétain was gone. Some say his hand was too heavy in France and he needed to go no matter what.

I arrived in Hamburg, Germany's great seaport. Unlike the somnolent Rhine Valley, Hamburg was bustling, the docks filled with tall stacked steam ships and oilers, with a dozen more waiting their turn to dock to unload their cargo. One saw ships from all over the world. Quite a few British-flagged vessels were docked or at anchor in harbor, a portent for things to come with the long term general thawing of Anglo-Germanic relations. Most interestingly, an American battleship lay at anchor.

I got off the train and found a hostel in which to stay the night. It was the kind of ramshackle two story establishment frequented by sailors and other transients. Ownership decorated the lobby with postcards from around the world and photographs of old ships. I got a small room, little more than a bed, table and chair and left my small suitcase there.

Sketchbook in hand I walked the waterfront taking in the air and feel of the place. I was most interested in the American battleship laying at anchor. I found a few crates and sat. There I had an excellent view of the ship, perhaps five hundred meters down river. I made a quick sketch of the ship, catching the two tall masts amidships and emphasizing the large guns forward. She was a sight for sure. As I went about my business, a launch came from the ship and landed a half dozen American sailors. They seemed to be waiting for something. Clad in blue dungarees, the sailors had deep lines and faces weathered by years of sea spray. Life in the navy turned their arms spindly and sinewy. They were all skinny, but each looked like he could lift a fifty kilo flour sack over his head with little effort. They milled about, chatting or smoking. One of them saw me sketching and walked over. He said something to me but I did not yet speak English. I held up my hands and said, 'Nein English.'

One of his fellow sailors approached and said, 'He wants to know what you are doing.'

'You speak German?' I asked.

'Ja,' the sailor said. 'I was born in Lubbock.'

'Wonderful,' I said. I turned my sketch to the Americans and showed them the sketch I made.

'Hey fellas, get a look at this!' The older sailor waved his friends over. The Americans gawked at the sketch I made of them. They all seemed amused by my work.

I tore the paper out of my sketch book and handed it to the older sailor. 'Please, be my guest,' I said.

'Hey, thanks?' he said.

I asked, 'Would you like another sketch? Perhaps portraits?'

The older sailor translated. The men looked at one another and nodded. 'Five marks each,' I said.

The older sailor reached into his pocket and took out a wad of green bills. 'All we have is Yankee dollars.'

I looked at the notes and shrugged. 'Why not?'

In this manner I made 30 American dollars for my trip.

The next day, suitcase in hand, I walked down the docks till I found the *Baltic*. She lay in the slip, many people walked her decks. Across the gangway leading up to her, a porter carried several suitcases. These were old and beat up. One was just a simple box held together with string. Right away I recognized them as the suitcases of my fellow artists, for only an artist would use an old box as a suitcase. At the gangway stood several sailors, a ship's officer in a white uniform, and a tall, black- haired bearded man who would soon become a dear friend. This was the great etcher, Hermann Struck. I approached and introduced myself.

Struck greeted me jovially, 'Ahhh, yes, of course!' He turned to a sailor holding a ledger and told him to strike my name off the list. He shook my hand. 'Won't you please come aboard?'

'I would be delighted,' I said.

'I am looking forward to seeing you aboard,' Struck said.

'As am I.'

The white-uniformed officer said, 'Won't you please leave your suitcases here, mein Herr?'

I did so and was shown to my cabin by a young English lad. Since I as yet spoke no English and he spoke no German, he showed me to my cabin without a word. Then he held out his hand in expectation of a tip. I gave him one of the American dollars I'd been paid earlier. He held the note in both hands and examined it. Determining the note was real, he pocketed the dollar and thanked me. The cabin was simple enough, a single bed, desk, chair and portal, comfortable for the trip, it would be.

We departed that afternoon. The *Baltic* sailed up the Weser and into the North Sea. For the first time I saw the sea. The vastness was breathtaking. I stood on deck for an hour just taking in the great, roiling blue expanse. The way the white caps appeared and then disappeared, but always in a pattern, the way the sun glinted off the water and how the rays looked different from different angles. I retrieved a sketchbook from my cabin, sat on a deck chair and sketched what I saw, the vast blue ocean, the sun lording over all. Later that night while other persons on board were dining and drinking and talking about our craft, I filled in the colors from memory.

Strange surroundings and the rolling sea made for a rough night's sleep. Despite waking up tired I looked forward to the day. Our scheduled event was a presentation by Hugo Vogel, already a legend by 1920 for the series of paintings he made chronicling Hindenburg's great victories in the east. He brought with him several prints. Vogel's works were impressive, of course.

I most enjoyed his painting of Hindenburg and Ludendorff at Tannenberg, Hindenburg before Vilnius, Pritwitz at Minsk and of course his series of portraits of the great Hindenburg himself. But more interesting than his work was Vogel's recollections of working with Hindenburg.

The general dominated every room, Vogel said. Greatness seemed to radiate from the man. Despite his great visage, he had the discipline to remain still as Vogel painted him. For two hours Hindenburg would sit and discourse on issues at hand, his thoughts on the post-war world and such. Hindenburg was very exacting. Vogel told us that time and again Hindenburg demanded changes of the most subtle nature. Hindenburg was determined to make sure he was painted in proper uniform, down to the buttons, their placement and color. We artists laughed at this, as we were used to painting for demanding clients. After a time, our little colloquium broke up for lunch. I dined by myself on a light lunch. As I finished my light meal, Hermann Struck approached.

'May I sit?'

I motioned to the empty chair. 'Please.'

'Tell me,' Hermann asked. 'You sketch and paint pieces about the war, ja?'

'Most often,' I replied.

'I have seen them. Most depict scenes of glorious victory.'

'It is what the public wants.'

'Does painting help you deal with the trauma of war?'

I shrugged rather indifferently. 'I would not say I suffer from trauma. I was never shell shocked. I saw shell shocked Russian and French soldiers. I am not like them.'

'Of course,' Hermann said. 'But the war remains within you. It does with me.'

'I suppose.'

'Perhaps you would consider writing down your experiences and sharing them with the group?'

'I do not know about that...'

'Come,' Hermann said. 'We are all veterans here and we are all artists. I think sharing your experiences may help you.'

Again I shrugged indifferently.

'Why not try?' Hermann said. 'At least come to a session today.'

I agreed.

Hermann's little conclave of veterans met in the ship's bar. Already several beers were poured. A gray-haired man missing his left arm offered me a beer, but politely I declined. I pointed to his stump. 'May I ask?'

'Ahhh,' he said. 'On the Marne. Where did you serve?'

'16th Reserve Infantry Regiment. In the East.'

'Come, mein Herr,' he said.

Perhaps a dozen men sat in a semi-circle, drinking, smoking and gabbing with one another. I sat quietly and watched. There I picked up snippets of conversation. My gray-haired, one- armed host talked of losing his arm at the battle of the Marne. When he was finished a sculptor with a young face but the eyes of a 50-year-old told of his time at the battle of the Seine. I listened with great interest.

'Ja, the Frogs had us under heavy fire. Many a man fell around me. But we kept dropping pontoons into the river, and slowly we got the pieces of the bridge assembled. As we did so, those fellows from the machinegun company advanced. With each section they came down the bridge, firing on the far bank.'

'Weren't you afraid?' my gray-headed host asked.

The man scoffed. 'I had no time for that. Later yes, but not as we were getting the pontoons in the water.'

'And what happened once the bridge was linked to the far shore?'

'Actually,' he said. 'I don't know. I recall standing in the Seine perhaps ten meters from the shore. The water was up to my waist. The commanders decided that was enough. So before the bridge was even completed, columns of men descended, jumped into the water and waded ashore. Those were some wet soldiers, let me tell you. Thousands must have gotten across before night.'

'Did you finish the bridge?'

He laughed. 'Nein. By then the troops had seized another crossing and there was no need.'

The assembled men clapped. My gray-haired host looked to me, nodded and introduced me. I stood, a bit uncomfortable before the men. And described the 16th RIR and our actions.

'What would you say,' asked my gray-haired host, 'was the most important action in which you took part?'

'Marching.'

Everyone else laughed. They all understood, of course

'Come now, seriously.'

I gathered my words, 'I was shelled and shot at now and again, but without a doubt the biggest action I took part in was at the village.'

'The village?'

Now it was my turn to laugh. 'Ah, ja. That is what I have always called the action. Just the village.'

'Well, what was the village called?'

I laughed. 'Now that I talk about it, I realize that I have no idea. Nobody ever told me the name.'

There were more laughs and guffaws and open hand slaps upon the table.

'We were south of Vilnius, before a small river…' I shook my head. 'Who knows? I suppose if I had a map I could find and name it.'

My gray-haired host said, 'Tell us about this battle.'

I searched for the words but found myself choking on them. My eyes teared up just a bit. I leaned forward.

'It is alright,'

'Ja, Ja…' I heard from the assembled.

'Do not push yourself.'

'We have plenty of time.'

'Perhaps,' said my gray-haired friend, 'you could write down your experiences and share them?'

I nodded. 'If you think it would help.'

'Ja, I do. In the meantime, just have a drink and chat with your fellow veterans.'

I ordered myself a beer. In all honesty I drank little of it and mostly listened. But I must say as the afternoon went on I felt more at ease, more so than I even did with the 1st Company during the war. I added a word here and there, but mostly I listened. I asked if anyone would mind if I sketched the scene. This was acceptable to a bar full of artists, of course. On a blank piece of paper I drew these men, grizzled veterans, all seemingly old, though none was over 30 except for our host. I have always liked the way my pencil captured the air, not just the cigar and cigarette smoke, but the sense of camaraderie and war that was hanging in the room.

That night I spent a few hours writing my account of the 1st Company's battle at the village. By the time I was finished the account went on for eight pages. Tired but fulfilled, I went to bed, prepared to read it to the conclave the next day. Hermann understood and did not bother me at all.

The next day I sat in a chair at the head of semicircle of vets. Without taking my eyes from the page I read what I had written about the village battle. I could only get to the part where we took the village. As I tried to read about the Russian counterattacks I paused, my voice became choked. My papers fell to the floor and I buried my face in my hands and sobbed. Several men got up and surrounded me. I felt hard, but warm comforting hands on my shoulders. Not since my mother had I felt so loved and cared for. I reached down and picked up my papers and sat back up. I cleared my throat.

'You do not have to go on.'

'No,' I said. 'I need to do this.'

With hands shaking and voice trembling, I read the entire memoir. Several times I stopped and wept, but each time I caught myself and read on. I do not know how long it took me to finish. Time seemed to simultaneously stop and move on with lightning speed. When I finished I looked up and the assembled artist veterans clapped. I stood slowly, clicked my heels and bowed, brushing the tears away. I sat and ordered a drink. This time I finished my beer.

Later I sat in my cabin, rethinking the afternoon, pondering what I felt about it. Frankly I was not sure. Hermann came by to see if I was unwell.

I thought back to the last few days and nodded, 'Ja,' I said. 'I am well.'

In truth I do not think I had felt that good since that afternoon in Marienplatz in Munich during the Great War rally. I felt almost exuberant after sharing my war story.

Between these sessions there was little to do during our week-long journey. To pass the time Hermann encouraged me to learn English. He spoke the language and offered to teach me. I agreed and daily he gave me lessons. I was always a quick study and by the time we reached New York I was able to 'get by'. That is, I could ask directions, order dinner and such. I tested my English skills on the American crew members. One morning I saw a sailor washing down the deck. He was an affable fellow clad in white pants and short sleeve shirt. Those sleeves revealed dark blue tattoos on his arms. Each was the silhouette of a ship with the name stenciled below. I pointed to those and asked. 'You serve in America's…' I searched for the word but could not find it, 'Kreigsmarine.'

He smiled. As an old sailor he knew the word Kreigsmarine, 'Navy.'

'Ah.'

'The United States Navy.'

'That is the word…navy.'

'Yeah,' he said. 'I was in till last year.'

'How long?'

His face came alive. 'Twenty-five years.'

'And then you leave? Why?'

'After the Mexico thing.'

'Mexico thing…oh yes.'

'I was at Vera Cruz. I even led a detachment ashore to bail out those marines. I remember thinking, as I pulled a gun out of a ditch, Jesus, I'm a navy man! So when that little party was over in 1919…' He paused. 'I'm sorry am I going too fast?'

In truth he was and he lost me with 'bail out' but I said 'Nein, please continue…'

'I took my pension and got out.'

We chatted amicably for a few more minutes before he went on with his duties.

The next morning we were all aboard the bow and we saw it, New York City. It was a wonderful scene, the Statue of Liberty, the Manhattan skyline, the Brooklyn Bridge. I had read before about the feelings of immigrants upon seeing the great port for the first time. Now I understood them. Most perhaps saw the future. But as our ship approached the Hudson River and the pier where we would dock for the night I saw the gateway to a vast continent. I could almost feel my spirit traveling up the great river then to the Mohawk to the Great Lakes and from there, to the American west.

Our ship docked on Manhattan's west side. Most of my fellow artists were excited to go ashore and experience New York City. I must admit I was more interested in sailing north. I thought I would remain aboard, but Hermann coaxed me out of my cabin. That evening we walked the streets. I had never seen anything like it. The people here, New Yorkers they call themselves, are variously and indifferently dressed. They move seemingly in all directions at once at a frenetic pace utterly foreign to Germany. Despite being a thousand miles away from a foreign city, New York City is the most international place I have ever been. The number of languages and accents here put Vienna to shame. In some ways New York City mirrors Vienna, for on the streets of Manhattan I heard Polish and Hungarian and Italian, much Italian. Almost as ubiquitous as Italian is German. Indeed, parts of Manhattan have a decidedly German feel. I was oddly comforted to walk down Fifth Avenue and hear two men speaking German, even if they do so in Saxony accents.

Also I saw Negroes for the first time. I had expected to see great black, towering physical specimens, but the Negroes here seemed of average build for an American. Also disappointing was their complexion. They were hardly dark at all, at least not by the standards of photos of French Senegalese prisoners I had seen. I asked Hermann about this and he explained that the Negroes here were the descendants of slaves and the result of what American southerners call 'nighttime integration'. At this I laughed.

Manhattan itself was most interesting. The southern tip of the island almost resembles a European city with its mismatch of winding, narrow streets. But once one moves north, the island is admirably laid out in a perfectly symmetrical grid of streets and avenues. The citizens of New York have even set aside a large tract of land in the middle of the island for a Central Park. I was also surprised to see some architectural masterpieces in a city that barely a century before was a fraction of the size it was in 1920. Here was wonderful Pennsylvania Station, a massive piece of neo-classical architecture, a throwback and tribute to our Greek and Roman forbearers. The station takes up two entire city blocks. Though the station's designers drew heavily from the Gare d'Orsay in Paris, they did not over-decorate as the French would have. Instead the granite edifice and columns stand on their own greatness without being swathed in French frippery. Inside is a great arched waiting room held up by massive stone columns.

One great rail station is not enough for New York. The city needs two. Not far from Penn Station is Grand Central Terminal and it dwarfs Penn Station. Grand Central handles New York's subway traffic. It opened in 1871 and was rebuilt just before the war. Here again the Neo-classical style reigns supreme and in redesigning the terminal the New Yorkers eschewed the more elaborate decorative pieces of the original structure and decided upon a more sensible and utilitarian structure. Gone are the original towers and porticos in favor of simple columns, large U-shaped windows and simpler edifices. Here I must say the American vision is most sound.

Overall Hermann and I spent a glorious day in Manhattan. By the time we returned to the ship I regretted that we would depart early the next morning.

Under a gleaming morning sun poised over the Atlantic Ocean and bathing lower New York in orange-pink light we steamed up the mighty Hudson River. When I first set eyes upon the Rhine I thought I would never see a more impressive waterway. Ha! The Rhine is a mere stream compared to the mighty Hudson. When we set out, the river was nearly a mile wide. As we steamed north it widened to two and eventually thee miles breadth. Once we sailed past Manhattan, hills lined the right bank. Upon these sat small river towns, Yonkers, Hastings, Tarrytown, Ossining, Croton and such. The towns began at the river bank and wound their way up the hilly slope. These all had small dock-strewn marinas filled with small merchant ships or pleasure boats. On the left bank lay a truly impressive geologic feature, the Palisades. These are vertical rock cliffs lining the bank of the river for nearly twenty miles north of New York City. The massive façade seems as if it was cleaved by the great Norse gods in a fit of rage. As we steamed north I could not move my eyes from them and made a quick sketch.

Across the river from Fort Washington, the scene of a great battle in the American Revolution, operatives of the Republican political party have erected a great sign that spells out P-E-R-S-H-I-N-G. The letters are in olive drab and khaki and nearly ten meters high. They could be seen from the New York side and all along the river. This, I was told, was a presidential campaign sign.

Indeed, the Americans' election was just six weeks away. Our guide informed me that General Pershing was the choice of their Republican party. This made sense to me, he was the victor of Mexico after all.

Eventually we rounded a cape into what the Dutch used to call the Inland Sea. Its great circular bowl surrounded by high, wooded ground on all sides. It was a lovely place to take a pleasure cruise and I wished our own ship would lounge there for a day or two so that we could take in and explore the site. We pushed on though, rounding another bend, this one amusingly called Anthony's Nose and then Bear Mountain. Here the Hudson narrowed to a more Rhine-like width, but was breathtaking nonetheless.

After passing Bear Mountain, I waited with anticipation for the great American Military Academy situated on the west bank. We were in a straight-away now. It continued for about seven kilometers until the point approached. As we grew near, both banks of the river were marked by Pershing campaign signs, and on the far bank, across from the academy someone had erected a great sign to rival the one on the Palisades. Other signs dotted both banks. They proclaimed statements like, 'Victor of Vera Cruz' and 'Conqueror of Chihuahua'. One large banner commemorated the 'March on Monterey'. Below that stood one lonely sign defiantly proclaiming, 'Viva Villa!' Then West Point came into view. The academy occupies commanding heights on the Hudson, and it is plain to see why the great George Washington erected a post here, and why the British were so eager to seize it. From our ship one could see several great gothic buildings built during the 19th century as well as the parade ground.

That night at dinner Hermann remarked on the academy and those at our table expressed admiration that a nation so young can possess such an obviously impressive military academy. Since I was the resident expert on architecture, Hermann asked for my thoughts. I replied that I had few to offer.

Later Hermann asked me 'Tell me, have you thought about doing more sketches of your experience in the East.'

'No,' I replied. 'I made many sketches on the front.'

'So why not make some more now?'

'I have preferred to move on,' I replied.

'You may find doing so cathartic.'

'I am afraid I have little to paint that would interest the public.'

'What do you mean?'

'The public wants to see and hear about glorious bayonet charges and victory parades.'

Hermann nodded. 'So they do.'

'I am afraid my paintings would contain nothing of the kind.'

'Perfect, then,' Herman says.

'I do not understand.'

'Right now the government is bombarding the public with celebratory art, is it not?'

I thought back to the streets of Berlin. Seemingly every home had a German flag in the window, every news vendor sold copies of the Treaty of Strasbourg. Children played army in the streets and got into arguments over who had to be the French or Russians.

'Ja.'

'So eventually that market will be flooded.'

'I suppose.'

'...and someone will want to see a different, dare I say more realistic portrayal of what went on during the war.'

I nodded my head. 'I suppose you are correct.'

'And when that moment arrives, the public will snap up your book.'

'My book?'

'I have seen your work. It is competent. And that inherent grimness in your work will complement the subject.'

Immediately I sensed what he meant. 'You know, you are right.'

Hermann slapped me on the shoulder, 'So get to work...'

CHAPTER 7

1964

———

WITH AN OLD COPY OF my *War Sketches* book under my arm, I arrive at the Bakers' door and politely knock. I hear the urgent patter of feet and then the door opens. Standing there is a young version of Aggie. The little girl's front teeth are missing and her hair is tied up in pigtails. Erica makes a great show of introducing herself and inviting me in.

'Welcome to our home,' she says.

'Danke,' I say.

'Bitte!' she exclaims. Erica turns to her mother and shouts, 'Mommy we're speaking German!'

'Erica, don't pester our guest. Won't you please come in?' Aggie asks.

I bow my head and thank her.

'Please sit.'

Aggie gestures to the couch. I sit and find it unusually soft and cushy. Americans and their comforts…

She looks at the old book under my arm, 'What is this?'

I hold it up and say, 'Your husband tells me you are an artist. I thought I would bring over a copy of my old book of war sketches.'

Aggie takes the book and flips through a couple of pages. 'Oh, how nice,' she says. 'I would love to have a real artist comment on his work with me.'

'Well, plenty of commentary is written below each sketch and in the introduction.'

Aggie flips to the front of the book. 'Hermann Struck' she reads.

'Ja, he was an etcher, for a time the Kaiser's etcher. He was my mentor, actually.'

'He helped you?'

'Oh yes,' I reply. 'To this day I do not know exactly what strings he pulled, but I know for a fact he helped get my book to the publisher.'

'He must really have admired your work.'

'He did, I am fortunate. That book sold well. The Kaiser even received a copy.'

'Oh my!' Aggie says.

Aggie places the book on the table and excuses herself to the kitchen. As Aggie readies a tray of tea and cookies, Erica regales me with her great adventure moving from America to Germany, telling me how friendly everyone is and how she was really sad to leave her friends in America but now that she's here she knows she'll make lots of friends and already wants to stay in Germany for the rest of her life.

'I'm sorry,' Aggie says as she walks into the drawing room.

I smile and take a cup of tea. As I heap a big spoonful of sugar into the saucer I reply, 'Not at all.'

'Mom! Mom!' Erica jumps up and down. 'We spoke German!'

Aggie sits and says, 'She's very excited to learn German.'

'I am happy to help if she likes and you will allow.'

'Please, you do not have to do that.'

Erica begged, 'Please! Please! Please!'

'It would be my pleasure. So, Frau Baker,' I ask, 'What do you think of Germany?'

Erica jumped up and down, 'I love it! I Love it! I love it!'

'Erica, please…' Aggie says. She was becoming impatient. 'So far the people have been friendly and helpful.'

'I am glad to hear that.'

'Everyone tells me how much they like Americans.'

'Of course.'

'Please, I know we can be loud and obnoxious.'

Aggie is right of course. I would never insult her countrymen in her home. I search for a way to change the subject and see an idealized portrait of their President Kennedy hanging on the wall. It is a rough sketch colored in earthy hues. The president sits at his desk in the oval office. He looks off in the distance presumably pondering the great issues of the day.

I point to the portrait and say, 'You are admirers of President Joseph Kennedy, ja?'

Aggie's face lights up. 'Oh yes, very much so.'

Erica rolls her eyes and says, 'Mommmm…you always talk about him.'

Aggie blushes. 'I admit I do.'

'Ah,' I sip my tea. 'And how do you think he is performing?'

'Oh, I think the President is wonderful.'

'I have not been following the American news very closely of late,' which was true. As with the rest of Germany, I've been paying attention to the Great War celebrations. 'What has he done?'

Aggie actually blushes, 'Well right now he is trying to push a Voting Rights bill through congress.'

'Voting Rights bill?'

'You know a bill to guarantee the right to vote for Negroes?'

Aggie explains to me the Jim Crow laws in the American south made to prevent Negroes from voting.

'I see, and your Congress is trying to put an end to this.'

'Trying, is the operative word.' Bitterly Aggie sips her tea.

'I have a Negro friend at home!' Erica proclaims.

Aggie pats her daughter's head.

I admit that the intricacies of the American government are not my strong suit. 'Why does this Voting Rights Bill not become law?'

Aggie grew irritated. 'The Southern Democrats are blocking it because they don't want Negroes to vote and the Republicans are holding it up because they are afraid the bill will give millions of new voters to President Kennedy.'

'Hmmmm,' I say. 'Why?'

'Most Negroes who can vote will do so for Democrats.'

'That seems strange to me,' I say. 'Was not your President Lincoln a Republican?'

Aggie seemed to ignore my question.

'So the Republican party worked very hard to keep this upstart Senator from getting their nomination.'

'Who?'

'A senator from Arizona.'

'I have been to Arizona,' I offer but Aggie was not interested.

'Barry Goldwater,' she almost spits out the name. 'He's pledged to undo the New Deal.'

'Ahhhh,' I nodded. 'The New Deal. I am a great admirer of your President Roosevelt's works. The TVA, the Hoover Dam. Good for the people to work.'

'I always thought so. The grandees in the GOP all got together and quashed Goldwater...'

'Our bergers and junkers would have done the same...'

'And they nominated the governor of New York, Nelson Rockefeller.'

'And he is not one of these Republicans against the New Deal?'

'No. But if millions of additional Negroes vote this year...'

I finished for her,'...then the advantage gained will negated.'

'Yes.'

'Ahh,' I nodded, 'good strategy.'

'I'm sorry?'

'Oh, I mean good strategy on the part of the Republicans to hold this Voting Rights bill until after the election.'

'Strategy?' Aggie replies, incredulity rising in her voice. 'We are talking about people being oppressed and you are talking about political strategy?'

It is now clear to me that I have offended Aggie without intending to do so. I notice that Erica leaves the room and realize in a moment, why.

'I mean, I guess it is too much to expect Germans to understand the civil rights struggle in the United States, not after what you did in the Congo.'

She is of course referring to the recent Congo crisis. Aggie goes on about this for nearly a minute, a stream of consciousness, almost random sentences strung together. I am hard-pressed to keep up. When she finally ceases, awkward silence fills the room. I finish my tea and stand.

'I have offended you, Aggie, my apologies.' I bow. 'I shall leave you now. Thank you for the tea.'

'Oh, I'm sorry,' Aggie says. 'Please don't go.'

'I think it is best.'

I say goodbye and went back to my apartment.

Back there I go over the conversation and my words, wondering if I said anything to upset Aggie. I hear a knock on the door. Aggie is there. She looks near to tears but was doing well controlling them.

'I'm so sorry,' she says.

'Please, come in.'

Erica walks past me and begins inspecting my apartment looking at my easel and paints and flipping through a series of postcards on which I had been working.

'Erica …' Aggie says to her daughter. She turns to me. 'I'm sorry for yelling at you.'

'Please, it is nothing. I accept your apology.'

'It's just that I have a good reason to be upset...'

Aggie seems like she wanted to tell me something.

I invite Aggie to sit on the couch.

'Mommy look at all his paint!'

'Erica!' she exclaimed.

'Nein, nein, it is fine.' I turn to Aggie. 'Would you like to paint something?'

'Yeah!'

I get an old canvas and place it on the easel and put several paints on a pallet for Erica. I show her how to hold the pallet but she says rather testily, 'Mommy already showed me.'

'Ahh...of course,' I smile. Erica takes the brush and gleefully goes to work splattering the canvas. In moments she turns into Jackson Pollack, whose work is on par with Erica's.

'You are very kind,' Aggie says.

'Nein, nein, it is my pleasure.'

Aggie says, 'I'm sorry I became so upset. It's just that in college I was a Freedom Rider.'

'Freedom Rider?'

'Activists who went down south to register Negroes to vote.'

'I see.'

'I got harassed, intimidated by thugs.'

'A most unpleasant experience.'

'I was in a few protests and got sprayed by a water cannon.'

'Water cannon?' I suppress a bit of sarcasm, I know this has obviously been difficult for Aggie. But invoking the trauma of a water cannon makes me think of being bombarded by a real cannon.

'Well, it appears soon your goal will be realized, with this Voting Rights Act.'

Personally I have always been indifferent to the Negro question whether in America or our own German colonies, but any fool should be able to see that the tide of racial equality, at least in the American south is unstoppable and would soon sweep away all these holdouts.

'I suppose you're right.'

'But then there will be much work to do for their social equality.'

'Social equality?"

'Racism, school segregation and the like. You know, equality.'

Inwardly I scoff at the notion that the negro is the equal of the white man, but I sense this is no time to argue about that. I nod and pat Aggie's knee.

She says, 'And I'm sorry to have criticized you about the Congo.'

I laughed. 'It is very well. The Congo can be a brutal place. I have seen so first hand.'

'Really?'

'Yes, in fact...'

CHAPTER 8

Munich, 1928

——

IT WAS A TRYING DAY. I had been painting the portrait of the teenage daughter of a wealthy Munich financier, Herr Weisethaller. The girl was lovely and a perfect subject. The same could not be said of her large, pushy mother who was demanding and unbearable. Walking up the stairs to my apartment I could still hear that fat woman, 'No, no…don't paint her with too much rouge…the light should play across Rachel's face more…no not like that…'

That apartment was in Prince Regent Square and I had lived there since my book of paintings commemorating the war sold tens of thousands of copies. The rent was several hundred marks per month and rightfully so. My apartment boasted a great entryway, three bedrooms, drawing room, kitchen and two baths. This was quite a step up from my pre-war Vienna flop-house days. Just furnishing such a fine apartment was a difficult task and I hired an interior decorator, Elsa Bruckman. She was the wife of a wealthy Munich socialite and publisher. On Frau Bruckman's advice I filled the apartment with austere and tasteful pieces from the Royal Bavarian Furniture Company. She made the drawing room the center of my home. In the middle was a round coffee table about which were gathered four low chairs and a pair of three-person couches. All had green flowered upholstery. A pair of couches were up against each wall and a chair by each entrance. One wall had a floor-to-ceiling book case housing my library of more than 300 books on art, architecture, history and philosophy.

My valet left a bundle of letters from the mail slot. These would be bills, fan mail, perhaps a solicitous offer for a portrait or a landscape. I looked at one envelope and saw the name Julius Graff Von Zech. It was a name I had not said in a decade. Intrigued I opened and read.

Greetings to my old comrade in arms. I hope this letter finds you well. I am writing because I understand you have become something of a successful artist and I have work for you, if interested. A colleague of mine serves with the Colonial Office in Congo and they would like to commission an artist to do a series of paintings for a promotional brochure. My colleague asked if I knew anyone who might be amenable. Given your recent work and our past relationship, I at once thought of you....

With my trip to America being so personally and professionally successful, I immediately wrote back my agreement. Upon receiving my telegram, the Colonial Office politely inquired if I could leave in three days. I telegraphed my agreement. The Colonial Office took care of everything, leaving a ticket for me on the steamer *Germania* at Hamburg and arranging the train trip to Hamburg.

The trip from Berlin to Hamburg took most of a day. The fields were bursting with grain, potatoes, radishes, onions, beans and other staple crops. Indeed a rising German agricultural sector was replacing that of France and even competing with America and South America on the world market. Unlike 1914, automobiles filled the streets and not just in the big cities through which we passed. One saw a few automobiles in even the smallest hamlets. During my trip to America I saw Henry Ford's American Model T and admired it greatly - a simple, affordable car for the working man. Germany should have such a vehicle. But I have ridden in the competing Mercedes and BMW models, and the Model T cannot compare to the engineering and craftsmanship of these German masterworks.

The *Germania* was filled with German pleasure seekers, colonial hands and businessmen. The businessmen displayed the new wealth pouring into Germany in the last decade. I noticed ivory-topped canes were popular. But the colonial hands wore rugged clothes tailored for Congo: clipped trousers or shorts in the English style and open-collared shirts with the top button undone. Much to my surprise at least half of these old hands were French-speaking Belgians.

We steamed into the Channel, stopped off at Portsmouth and passed on through to the Atlantic. The following day we saw the African coast. I watched in fascination as we sailed past mile after mile of rocky beach. This was not the Darkest Africa of my imagination but a sun baked desert seemingly out of the Bible. The senses were bombarded by an explosion of yellows and browns ending in an ocean of blue water. It was quite the contrast of colors and I'd not seen anything quite like it before. On and on it stretched. My one hope was to see an Arab on the shore. And though I spotted many people, this was as close as we got. French Colonial authorities barred *Germania* or any other German ship from docking.

Marshall Pétain was in the 14th year of his 'presidency' though his rein was far closer to a military dictatorship. At least he did not style himself an emperor in the manner of the clown Napoleon III. Pétain's refusal to dock German ships came as a result of the instability of the French empire. Ever since the Treaty of Strasbourg, French colonial possessions had been wracked by one disturbance after the other. This varied from civil disobedience within its Southeast Asian possessions to outright revolt in North Africa. The Algerian crisis was then in its fifth year. The right wing in France believed the root of their trouble in Algeria grew from Berlin. The left in France was even more ridiculous, with the communists insisting that the Algerian revolt was a class struggle when even the Arab leadership insisted theirs was a struggle for nationhood. Honestly, I doubt the average Arab had even heard of Marx. His tirades against colonialism contained both folly and danger. What would the peoples of Africa do without the civilizing hand of the white man?

I would soon see why we were needed.

On the 5th day of the cruise we rounded the African hump and sailed across the continent's equatorial underbelly. I had never experienced heat quite like this. The combination of temperature and humidity produced an omnipresent steam that rose out of the very jungle. From a distance I spied Africans on the shoreline, though I am sorry to say I could distinguish little about them. We stopped at Togo, dropping off a few passengers and taking on a few more and did the same the next day at Cameroon. Once Togo had been a prestige colony, my old comrade Von Zech ran it after all, but now Togo was, as the Americans would say, 'old news'. Indeed the energy of German African colonialism had shifted to the great prize of the war, Congo.

That night our ship lay at anchor at the mouth of the Congo River. In the morning a launch came up to *Germania's* side and disgorged two passengers, a river pilot and a burly, thick-necked man who it turned out was looking for me. Upon finding me, he extended a beefy hand and said, 'My name is Horst Daly, I'm with the Colonial Office.'

'Pleased,' I replied. 'You are my guide, then?' I asked.

'Ja,' he replied. 'I will see you to Matadi, Wilhelmsville and the interior.' He pointed inside. 'Shall we have a seat?'

'If you like,' I said.

We sat in one of the ship's drawing rooms. Horst's large frame filled up the chair. I ordered tea, Horst a morning wine. He held up his glass, 'When one spends as much time with these French speakers as I, one picks up their habits.'

Horst asked after my accommodations and then began business, 'So, we'll take you up river to Wilhelmsville. After a night there, a grand tour of some of the Congo's industries. You may sketch whatever you like, of course.'

'That is good.'

'We should like to commission several formal paintings.'

'Certainly.'

'We shall pay you for each painting. These will eventually go in Congo brochures and such.'

I nodded in agreement.

I felt the ship get underway.

Horst held up his glass and drank. 'You, my friend, are in for quite a sight; the wonders and splendor of Congo.'

We sailed into the mighty Congo, gateway to darkest Africa. Here the river mouth was wide and deep, dwarfing the Rhine and even the great Hudson River. A midsized port lay on the Congo's South bank. We passed it without fanfare and proceeded up river. There was little sign of habitation on either bank. I was impressed with the rich, deep vegetation and got the sense of being surrounded by green. Never in Germany or America had I seen a green so vibrant, healthy and powerful. It seemed as if the very jungle would leap off the river banks and engulf us. We encountered only a few major settlements, first the small town Boma on the north bank and then Matadi, a midsized town. Here the Congo River turned sharply north toward the interior and narrowed considerably. Just beyond Matadi were rapids impassable to river traffic. The next 200 kilometers we would cover via railroad.

The railroad followed the river north and east. Brush and low vegetation covered the bank but beyond was the same lush, fertile green jungle we saw earlier. Low jungle covered hills on either side of us. Every few miles we passed a small village. These were straw and thatch huts with dugout boats on the river banks. I saw natives sitting on the river bank or tending to their boats. Children ran to and fro as did women, mostly topless in fact. How my old comrades in the 16ᵗʰ RIR would have hooted at such a sight! The women had great blankets wrapped around their heads, and often, a baby strapped to their back in a similar garment.

I remarked to Horst, 'We have not seen a white person since Matadi.'

'Nor will you,' Horst replied.

'Really?' I said. 'There are no whites out here?'

'Not in the villages, unless needed. Our people stay in the big cities and towns, or the plantations. What need is there for a white presence in these insignificant little villages?'

'Ah,' I nodded. 'But I thought missionaries were at work in the country?'

Horst laughed. 'Missionaries? Here? Have you seen poles sticking out of the ground, or the water?'

Now that Horst mentioned it, I had. Quite prominently in fact.

'Those have ju-ju.'

'Ju-ju?'

'Ju-ju offerings to their gods. Or spirits, really.'

'Really?'

'Yes. They make an offering to their water spirit for a plentiful catch. Or an offering to the baby spirit for a boy.'

'I see.'

'Outside of the cities and larger towns everywhere you will see ju-ju. Much ju-ju.'

I shrugged. Was this ju-ju really any different than the act of holy communion? To me it was all primitive superstition.

Near evening we rounded a bend and entered Wilhelmsville. Here one saw the hand of the white man. A great two story customs house lay on the waterfront. Next to the customs house was a dock and several open-aired warehouses. Beyond these was a city of one and two-story structures. Here finally I saw whites, many of them. The workers at the train station were white, mostly Belgians I was surprised to learn, save for the dozens of black porters carrying luggage or working in the station. Horst led me out front where several motorcars waited.

He raised his hand and whistled. One car pulled forward.

'I telegraphed ahead. This is a Colonial Office car.'

We drove out of the station and through dusty streets. The streets carried automobiles - all driven by Europeans. There were many blacks but not dressed as the ones I saw on the Congo River. These were westernized, right down to their short haircuts and manner.

We drove to the Hotel Metropole. Horst explained, 'The Colonial Office keeps a suite of rooms here for visitors and dignitaries. We shall lodge here for the night.'

I nodded appreciatively.

I was surprised that the hotel had kept its Belgian name and further surprised to find it kept its Belgian staff. An old Walloon doorman greeted us and sent us to the desk attended by a Mssr. Van der Vuys. He knew Horst and chatted amiably with him before ringing up a pair of black porters. They were impressive men, tall and broad chested, like the very idea of the noble savage. However they wore shorts, knee socks and buttoned-down short sleeve shirts. Both greeted Horst respectfully and took our bags. We walked across freshly waxed hardwood floors and passed rattan furniture. Fans swirled above, offering relief from Congo's heat. At the foot of the stairs was a portrait of the Kaiser, the only indication that we were in German territory. Otherwise the walls were decorated with antique maps of Congo, photographs of King Leopold, even a framed Belgian flag. I laughed and said, 'Looking around, one wonders who won the war.'

We stepped onto an elevator. Here a young boy similarly appointed as our porters greeted us. 'I am surprised you allow them to keep the hotel Belgian.'

Horst replied, 'Except for the director, the hotel is staffed and run by Belgians. They are loyal to the company. Why antagonize them?'

I nodded.

Indeed, as we toured over the next few days, I found that except for a few Germans, a plantation director, or a chief constable, the entire colony was run by Belgians. It is almost as if we colonized the colonizers. I suppose we had. My room was well appointed and otherwise comfortable. I slept under mosquito netting, a new experience for me. They buzzed throughout my room, the ceiling fan twirling above did little to disperse them. I thought after my time in the army I could sleep anywhere under any conditions, but not here.

After a long night Horst and I met for breakfast. In the dining area sat a few Belgian colonial policemen, a planter and a few German salesmen.

I made do with toast and tea. Being a large man, Horst indulged in eggs and sausage and *pommes frites.*

Between bites, Horst briefed me on Congo's economic situation.

'Look,' he said, 'as you can see, this is still a Belgian colony.'

I bit my toast and nodded.

'We rule here now, but the day-to-day operations are run by the Belgians who were already here. After the treaty, most stayed behind with their livelihoods.'

'Understandable.'

'So, you will meet many Belgians or other people who are not necessarily loyal to the Reich.'

I nodded.

'Which is not to say that they make trouble. They do not. Just try to avoid mentioning the war.'

'I shall do my best.'

After breakfast Horst took me by motorcar around Wilhelmsville. The town was founded by the great Lord Stanley at the behest of King Leopold for whom it was originally named. Belgian authorities managed the growth of Wilhelmsville, laying out the town in an orderly grid, so unlike the haphazard cities of Europe. The buildings were built in the French tropical style, with large porches and porticos so the white citizens could enjoy the cool night air. The Belgians still stubbornly call the place Leopoldville.

It was on this drive that I composed my first sketch, a quick drawing of a lumber company headquarters. After that, Horst asked if I would mind sketching the great Congo River waterfront. I agreed. We drove down to the Congo River. Here was a great inland port facility. The products of the empire packed the docks. On one dock sat a mountain of coffee bean crates, on another a sea of white ivory. In the water next to another dock were great cords of lumber from the interior. All these goods were moved about or tied down by native porters, blacks much darker than the negroes I saw in America. Most wore western style trousers but did not bother with shirts in the African heat. Here and there was a white overseer in charge of it all. These inevitably wore trousers and a white shirt with sleeves rolled up. Atop a head close-shaved against the heat sat a pith helmet or bush hat. Curiously, as I watched I heard no German spoken, only Flemish-French.

'Truly, this is still a Belgian place.'

'As I said, mein Herr, we have colonized the colonizers.' Horst looked over my shoulder. 'You are making this scene come alive.'

'You are too kind.'

'It will be an excellent piece for the brochure.'

'Danke,' I said.

'Would you like to sketch some of the natives?'

'Ja, ja!' I replied.

Horst went over to one of the overseers on the ivory-choked dock and explained who I was. The overseer whistled and called a half dozen coolies over. He spoke the local lingo, and pointed to me. Horst said something, the overseer nodded and spoke to the coolies, who then each picked up an ivory tusk. So appointed, Horst led them over to me.

'What language is that?' I asked.

'Lingala,' said Horst. 'It is prominent here but not in the interior.'

'The ivory is a most interesting detail,' I said.

'I thought so. Please make sure it is prominent,' said Horst.

I laughed.

'What is funny?' he asked.

I told him of my recent experience with Frau Weisethaller.

'So we are all demanding, then!'

I laughed again.

I nodded to the great black men. They were young, and stout, and strong, their sinewy muscles made taut by the labor of carrying the tusks. They smiled and spoke Pidgin French to me. The coolies stood passively as I sketched them. When I was finished I showed them the sketch. They smiled and nodded. Horst gave each man a reichsmark for their trouble and dismissed them. He looked at my sketch.

'Ja, that is perfect. It will give the brochure an exotic feel.'

'An interesting study,' I said. 'I should like to do more of this kind in Wilhelmsville.'

'Of course,' Horst said. 'But tomorrow I would like to take you out to one of the great elephant hunting grounds in the interior.'

I smiled, 'That sounds wonderful.'

With the sun high in the sky, the coolies on the overseer's orders broke for lunch and then a post-lunch siesta in the Spanish style. This was an excellent idea as I found the heat most draining and wanted nothing more than to wash away the layer of sweat and grit accumulated on my body. Horst took me back to the Metropole where I cleaned up and slept. Over dinner we discussed the next day's plans. As Horst ordered coffee he saw an acquaintance walk in. His face came alive. Horst whistled, pointed and waved. His acquaintance waved and pointed back. He tipped his bush hat and said, 'Ah, oui, Monsieur Horst.'

'That is Dupuy,' Horst told me as his friend came over. 'He owns a large plantation in the interior.'

Horst and I stood. He introduced me to Dupuy. I took his hand noticing that it was long, rough and bony. So, too, was Dupuy's face, tanned from the sun and featuring a handlebar mustache. He was taller than me, with long, powerful legs. His rolled-up sleeves revealed muscled arms beneath skin tanned and freckled by the Congo sun. Here was an impressive man and I was already glad to meet him.

He let go of my hand and bowed slightly. 'Ah,' Dupuy said, 'one of our German masters.'

'Do not mind him,' Horst said to me. 'Dupuy cannot help himself.'

'Not at all,' I said.

'In truth,' Horst went on, 'Dupuy could not care less who runs the Congo.'

'True enough,' Dupuy said, 'So long as I am left alone to run my planta-tion. Which I must say, has not been the case.'

'No?' Horst asked.

'Come to the bar, I shall tell you.'

Horst nodded to the maître d'.

'I am buying,' Dupuy said as he took a large roll of Belgian francs from his pocket. He nodded to me, 'And what does our resident artist drink?'

'In truth, I do not,' I confessed.

'Come,' Dupuy insisted, 'We are at a bar talking about the Congo.'

I shrugged but Horst saved me, 'Have a gin,' he said. 'The British say it helps with malaria.'

I agreed.

Horst ordered a beer while Dupuy asked for a bottle of whisky and a glass. Before I even sipped my gin, Dupuy polished off his glass and poured himself another.

'So what brings you to Wilhelmsville?' Horst asked.

'I have a meeting with the colonial governor.'

'Oh my,' I said.

Dupuy looked at me and said, 'I have much influence with him.'

I nodded in understanding.

'One of his colonial officers is annoying me.'

Dupuy explained. One of the Lingala-speaking tribes on the edge of his estate was making trouble, stealing cattle from his farm. Normally Dupuy and farmers like him handle these matters themselves without too much trouble. The theft was really a diplomatic ploy, more or less, where the chief wanted to come to an understanding on another matter, water or grazing rights or some such. More often than not the cattle are returned unharmed. But before Dupuy could enter negotiations with the chief, the local constable, a new man from Berlin, marched his policeman and constabulary right into the chief's village and demanded the return of the cattle. The chief agreed. Thinking he had won his first victory, the new constable was shocked the next day when the chief sent him the heads of the cattle. The new constable overreacted and seized some of the chief's own cattle as compensation to Dupuy.

'I refused, of course,' Dupuy said as he polished off another glass. 'And I chastised this constable.'

'Who?'

'Ruhn. Do you know him?'

Horst shook his head.

'I have dealt with Chief Ntema before. He is eminently reasonable. But not after this Ruhn buffoon.'

'It would seem not,' said Horst.

'So tomorrow I meet with the governor.'

'I doubt he will take any action,' Horst said.

'No. But my protest goes on record as does this idiot Ruhn.'

'Smart,' Horst laughs. 'He will not like Schmidt making this trouble any more than you do.'

'No,' Dupuy agrees. 'The less for him to do, the better.' He poured himself another glass. Self-consciously, I sipped my gin.

Horst said, 'Say, could we come to your plantation with you?'

Dupuy shrugged, 'If you like. Why?'

Horst patted my shoulder, 'Because my artist friend here should be on hand to chronicle your peace treaty with Chief Ntema.

Dupuy laughed. 'It is not all that. Peace treaty. . .' he shook his head.

'You don't mind going, do you?' Horst asked me.

'Not at all.'

In fact, I was intrigued by the notion of meeting some genuine African tribesmen. Already ideas were coming together in my mind. I saw sketches of plantation workers happy in their work, of native tribesmen clad in loin cloth and spear, of Dupuy and Ntema solemnly shaking hands. . .It was all there. These are the images that danced in my head as I went to sleep.

Dupuy spent most of the next day conducting business in Wilhelmsville. Horst took me to various Colonial Office installations throughout town, including its headquarters. I expected a great nerve center of colonial enterprise. Instead, the building was a simple, two story affair with the same veranda and portico as most of the other buildings in Wilhlemsville. Inside hung the air of an office where the boss is away on business. In fact, the governor was away inspecting some mines deep in Congo's interior. Half of the white staff were

Belgians well-acclimated to Congo. Some had been born there. These were wearing loose shirts and trousers and sandals. The Germans, I had learned, were easy to spot, insisting on Berlin formal wear despite the climate's complete inhospitality to suits. Overall, the office had a most un-German feel.

The next morning Dupuy met us in the lobby of the Metropole. Outside waited an open-topped motorcar and a soft-sided truck. A white man was behind the wheel of the truck and a coolie was seated in the passenger seat. Two more coolies were in the back, which otherwise was filled with crates. Dupuy drove his motor-car. A coolie waited in the passenger seat.

All morning we drove. Once outside of Wilhelmsville, the road was dirt - a well maintained path of sandy brown set against a barrage of green. The terrain was hilly but not mountainous. We passed other vehicles, trucks, police cars, and several times large trailers carrying massive felled trees. People walked along the road, too. These were always blacks, usually women carting water over their shoulders or carrying wicker baskets. More often than not a baby or small child was ingeniously tied down to the small of a woman's back. After a few hours we stopped for a lunch of sandwiches and crackers. Dupuy took his with whisky, a case of which he bought in Wilhelmsville. I ate sparingly just a few crackers and water though Dupuy insisted that I put a few drops of gin in my cup against the threat of malaria.

'From here,' he said, 'we shall turn east into the interior. If all goes well, we will make it to my plantation by dinner.'

Horst patted my shoulder and said, 'Ja, you will see the jungle.'

'This is not the jungle?' I motioned to the green all around us.

Horst laughed. 'This? This is sparse woodland. This is nothing. You shall see.'

Indeed I did.

Dupuy drove us into the interior. It was here that the phrase 'darkest Africa' took on real meaning for me. Along the sides of the road and above us, the trees formed a thick canopy that all but blocked out sunlight. The jungle enveloped us. I wondered how white men ever penetrated this awesome jungle. I thought of my Karl May novels and how the Americans referred to 'Indian country' for areas unsafe to travel. Naïvely I asked, 'Do we have to worry about the natives?'

Dupuy shook his head. Horst laughed and pointed to the crest on the motor car's door. It was a cocoa leaf and ivory tusk set against a blue *fleur-de-lis*. 'Not at all. You see that crest? Every native between here and his plantation knows Dupuy.' He patted Dupuy's shoulder. 'They know they can do business with Dupuy, here. And besides they know to leave the white man alone.'

In the passenger seat the coolie made a 'dit-dit-dit-dit' sound.

'What is he saying?' I asked.

Horst mimicked the coolie. 'Dit-dit…Maxim.'

I nodded in understanding; Maxim machinegun.

'I saw those for myself,' I said.

Horst said, 'So you know what they could do to the natives.'

'Ja.'

Dupuy said, 'We will avoid such necessity. I would much rather get on with these people. Better for them, better for me.'

After a few more hours Dupuy turned down a gravel pathway, it was barely a road. We went along at a mere 20 kilometers per hour, bouncing and rattling in our seats.

'I cleaved this path myself,' Dupuy bragged. 'My men and I mined the gravel from the river and laid it down. You should have seen the path before!'

The jungle opened up into a vast clearing. What a site! Before me was the very picture of a lush, prosperous plantation. A herd of cattle grazed lazily off to our left. Here were vast fields, one filled with cocoa, another with tea and a third with coffee. The fields ran right up to the manor house. This was a great wooden structure situated on a patch of high ground overlooking the plantation. Behind the manor house was a jungle-covered ridge running off into the northeast as far as I could see. Here and there, bits of the ridge had been clear-cut for lumber. As I looked wide-eyed at the vast plantation, Dupuy beamed with pride. The house was two stories with a great veranda before the front door, which was open, as were all the windows, though screens kept the mosquitos out. I smelled a meal in final stages of preparation.

A manservant in shorts, collared shirt and jacket waited at the top of the stairs. Dupuy got out of his car and walked up the stairs, handing his hat to the servant.

'Pleasant trip, Mr. Dupuy?' he asked.

'Yes, Tshombe,' he replied.

'And I see guests. Most excellent, Mr. Dupuy. Three for dinner then?'

'Yes,' Dupuy replied.

'There are several papers on your desk, Mr. Dupuy,' Tshombe said. 'One is a note from Captain Ruhn.'

'I'll look at them right away.'

'Yes, sir.'

'Please see to the guests.'

'Of course.'

Dupuy said, 'Please excuse me, gentlemen.'

'Right this way, sirs,' Tshombe said.

Inside, the house was ruggedly but comfortably appointed, with hardwood floors and rattan furniture. I appreciated Dupuy's utilitarian and minimalist tastes, necessary for the jungle, of course. A great fireplace dominated the main floor. Above this sat a map of Congo. I inspected it with great interest. The map was a work of art itself, with icons depicting lumber, minerals, rubber and other resources in the areas from which they came. An inset on the bottom left corner showed the Dupuy estate and boasted that it numbered 10,000 acres. Tshombe showed Horst and myself to a pair of guest rooms. Mine was small but comfortable and had a great window which opened up to the ridge. Immediately I saw great potential for a sketch. When Tshombe asked if I would like to freshen up before dinner, I asked for a bath. He had two coolies place a large tub in my room. As they filled it with buckets of warm water I sketched them both. Neither minded, gratefully accepted the coins I gave them for their trouble, and walked out facing me and bowing.

Dinner was served promptly at six. We sat at a long, mahogany table with straight-backed chairs, each decorated with the Belgian flag. Dupuy sat at the head of the table, Horst and I on either side. The rest of the table was empty, though it clearly was made for a large family. Dupuy changed into white slacks and button-down shirt and open-toed shoes, formal in its own right but very useful in the Congo heat. The chefs prepared a sumptuous feast that included beef, a boar hastily slaughtered for our benefit, yams, plantains and a variety of vegetables. Several kinds of alcohol were available, and I satisfied Horst with a gin-infused glass of water. Two servants, one an old man, one an adolescent boy, stood by. I had a bit of pork but helped myself to the generous servings of yams and plantains as I had never eaten these before.

As we dined Horst asked, 'So, what word from Ruhn?'

Dupuy took a long pull of port and said, 'He is an incompetent buffoon. He tells me that Chief Ntema refuses his demands.'

'What is he demanding?'

'The men who stole my cattle,' Dupuy replied. 'As if Ruhn does not understand that Ntema was present when the cattle were stolen. Idiot.' Dupuy drank again.

'Ja,' Horst said. 'A young officer trying to make a name for himself.'

'He is a fool. Why does Berlin send them here?' Dupuy looked at me. 'I am sorry to bore you with my troubles.'

'Not at all,' I said. 'Frankly these natives are most interesting.'

Dupuy said, 'My father built this plantation in the time of Leopold. I helped him.'

'And you do not now mind that Congo is German?' I asked.

'Germany, Belgium, it makes no difference. This place is African. This plantation is still here and it is still my home. If you ask me, I would prefer the Belgians to have stayed,' he said Belgians almost as if they are a foreign people, and I suppose that to him they are. 'My father and mother are buried outside our small chapel and so shall I be buried one day.' Dupuy slapped the table with an open palm. 'And one does not stay here 50 years, as we have, by antagonizing the blacks.' Dupuy cleared his throat. 'Look around,' Dupuy said to me. 'I have a white overseer yes, a few white mechanics and engineers, but everyone else here is black. I employ hundreds, thousands if one counts Ntema's tribesmen. We get on splendidly.' Dupuy polished off his port. 'But look at me going on.'

We finished our meal after which Dupuy invited us to the drawing room. Before the great fireplace he and Horst drank, I sketched. For entertainment he called in several adolescent boys. Clad in shorts and long button-down shirts they sang native tribal songs for our pleasure. 'This one is about the buffalo hunt,' Dupuy would say, or 'this one is about the elephants...' Their voices were as genuine and lovely as any in a German church choir. I sketched the marvelous scene. In this way we passed the evening. About ten o'clock, Dupuy said we would be starting out early in the morning and said he must get to bed and suggested Horst and I do the same. We both agreed. To my embarrassment Tshombe asked if we would require female companionship. I blushed and declined but Horst gleefully took Tshombe up on his offer. All night I listened to Horst frolic with his African girl. I must say I was most disappointed in Horst and told him so the next morning. He brushed me off without a care.

That morning was glorious, a beautiful mist hovered over the plantation and the dense jungle beyond. As the sun peeked over the horizon, the mist reflected the rays back into the sky, bathing us all in a yellow-white light. The sun's rays would not long be stopped, though, and soon the morning mist burned off. Around us, the plantation hummed to life. Dupuy's car was waiting out front. Horst and I got in the back as Dupuy's coolie loaded a few things into the trunk - coffee, tobacco and a few other odds and ends as a peace offering to Ntema. Dupuy came out and left instructions with his overseer, Jacque.

Dupuy got in the car and placed a rifle between himself and the coolie. I did not recognize the weapon and asked after it.

'This is a Krag,' Dupuy said.

'Krag?' I repeated.

'Krag-Jørgenson. Swedish-made but produced by the American Springfield armory. I have an armory full of them.'

'Are you expecting trouble?' Horst asked.

'Not especially. In this case the Krag is mostly for show. Besides, we might see a wild boar,' Dupuy patted his coolie on the back. 'Kwami here is an excellent shot..'

I was most taken aback by this. Dupuy trusts his black workers enough to arm them and commands their loyalty. Truly he must be a great leader.

We drove until we found Ruhn's encampment by the side of the road. This was a large tent, some collapsible chairs and tables and another tent in which slept a half dozen constables. Ruhn was easy enough to spot. He stood out in in his knee boots, billowed trousers and gleaming white shirt buttoned at the wrist and collar. Even I could tell he was not properly dressed for Congo.

Dupuy mocked, 'He must have read how the English say don't give into the heat and the heat will give in to you.' Dupuy shook his head. 'He is what the English would call a greenhorn.'

Dupuy got out of the car. Ruhn walked out of his tent and nodded to him. 'Guten tag,' he said.

'Do you speak English?' Dupuy asked.

'Ja.'

'Good, Herr Ruhn,' Dupuy said. 'You have caused much trouble for me with Ntema, you know that?'

'I have to enforce laws. This Ntema fellow stole your cattle.'

'Which I could have gotten back via a simple negotiation at the end of which he would have compensated me for the theft. He just wanted something. Now the cattle are gone and Ntema is angry with me.'

'I...'

'Really made a mess of this whole situation. Now I have to fix it.'

Ruhn had nothing to say.

One of the constables spoke in Pidgin French. I could not follow, but Dupuy understood him perfectly. 'What?' he said. 'Where?'

The constable pointed.

'Oh, lord,' Dupuy said.

Horst cursed.

Behind Ruhn's tent an African tribesman sat cross-legged and hand-cuffed. The right side of his face was red and bloated.

Dupuy said something in Lingala. The handcuffed man answered back.

'You idiot!' Dupuy said. 'That is Ntema's brother, Kama.'

There followed from Dupuy a most impressive string of curses and insults in at least three different languages ending with Dupuy demanding that Ruhn let Kama go. Ruhn feigned insult and asked after Dupuy's insolence.

Horst stood up in the car and pointed at Ruhn, 'Give him to Dupuy or I'll tell the governor about your buffoonery.'

'I am the duly appointed constable for this district.'

'I am the Colonial Office representative. I can see the governor whenever I like. And I would like to see him now so I may talk about you.'

'Why I...'

'Try me, Herr Ruhn….'

'Very well,' Ruhn said. 'If you want this savage, he is yours.'

Ruhn ordered one of his constables to uncuff Kama. Dupuy said something to him in his native language. Ntema's brother got in the car next to me without even acknowledging I was sitting there. He just stared forward, his face a mask. I looked the man over. He was an impressive specimen - thin and muscled, his skin taut. As he sat, I saw the beginnings of a stomach paunch, probably the result of his station in life. His facial features prominent and determined. His eyes dark and piercing. I was struck by the man's nobility, but also his dangerousness. Soon I would experience the latter.

We left Ruhn standing dumbfounded and having permanently lost the respect of his constables. Dupuy said something to Ntema's brother. Then he explained in English, 'We are taking him back to Ntema. That should calm things down and put me back in Ntema's good graces.'

Ntema waited just a few kilometers down the road with a coterie of men. As we approached, Ntema came forward. He was the same type as his brother, strong, stout, determined. In fact, the pair were physically indistinguishable - they were twins. As a mark of power and prestige Ntema actually wore a black button-down shirt, given to him by Dupuy. Ntema shouted something. I did not understand a word except 'Ruhn'. Ntema said the name again and made quick thrusting motions as if he were holding a spear. Dupuy said something back and pointed to Ntema's brother. He got out of the car and shouted, walked forward with hands held up high above his head. As he neared Ntema, his shouts became chants. Ntema shouted back. This was not the reunion between brothers I expected.

As the two brothers verbally confronted one another, Dupuy got back in the car and turned us around.

'Let us go,' he said. 'These two have to work things out.'

'What?' Horst asked.

'It seems Kama here says we brought him back because he used his….' Dupuy searched for the word, 'magic on us. Kama says he is a ju-ju man.'

Horst laughed.

'Come, now, Horst,' Dupuy said. 'You have been here long enough to know that these people take magic seriously.'

I asked, 'Does Kama really believe this?'

Dupuy said, 'While Ruhn was holding him, Kama probably invoked some spirit god to release him.'

'Ah-ha,' I said. 'And our arrival was this spirit's way of helping Kama.'

'In Kama's view, yes.'

I asked, 'So now Kama is challenging Ntema for leadership of the tribe?'

'With his new, powerful ju-ju, yes.'

Horst looked at me and said, 'So it seems you will see a native power struggle.'

So much for Rousseau's noble savage. These people were practicing the art of power as ruthlessly as anyone in Berlin or Vienna.

I shrugged. 'And I thought the American system was flawed.'

Horst laughed. 'It is better than measuring ju-ju power.'

I pondered ju-ju power on the ride back to the Dupuy plantation.

Over dinner Dupuy grumbled. 'That stupid Ruhn,' he said. 'Why do they send these nincompoops?' He cursed in French and shook his head. 'Berlin.'

Horst said, 'Now wait just a minute...'

Dupuy smiled. 'Apologies, mein Herr. I did not mean to insinuate that the Kaiser's government was anything but the most competent and efficient ever.'

Horst scowled at the obvious irony but was too polite to argue with our host.

'Brussels always left these matters to us,' he said. He sighed, 'Such is life.' Dupuy took a long swig of whisky.

Dupuy went on at some length about the various minor crises he had dealt with over the years. These ranged from water and grazing rights, to one incident before the war where Ntema asked Dupuy to keep a Christian missionary away from his tribe. Dupuy was going on at some length about that incident over coffee and tea when Tshombe politely entered the dining room and said, 'Excuse me sir, but Ntema's brother is here.'

'Here? What does he want?'

'Well, sir. He has brought some dozens of men with him. They are heading up the drive now.'

'They are coming to the house?"

94

'Yes, sir,' Tshombe replied most calmly. 'Mr. Jacque took the liberty of ordering all of the plantation hands to their quarters and to stay down.'

'That was very smart. Thank you, Tshombe.'

We got up and looked out the window.

There stood Kama with perhaps fifty men. All carried spears and wore red and yellow paint on their faces and across their chests. Dupuy peered at them and said 'Oh hell. That paint.'

Dupuy said, 'The red is for blood. The yellow is for the setting sun. Meaning that my time is over.'

Horst said, 'Not good.'

'Tshombe!' Dupuy shouted.

Tshombe hurried into the great room. 'Sir?'

'Get Kwami.'

'Yes, sir.'

Dupuy went to his study and got a set of keys. One opened the big gun locker he kept by the kitchen and the ammunition locker next to it. Inside were a half dozen Krag rifles. He looked at Horst and me.

'Can you two shoot?'

Horst nodded. I said, 'I was in the 16th Bavarian Reserve Infantry Regiment.'

Dupuy took one of the Krag rifles down and handed it to me. I looked the rifle over. Unlike my old Mauser it had a beach on the side of the receiver where rounds were inserted.

'You can use it, yes?' Dupuy asked.

'Ja,' I replied.

Dupuy took a box of ammunition and opened it. He took a handful of rounds and handed them to me. I took one and loaded it into the magazine and then another until it was full. Horst did the same.

Tshombe looked out the window, 'They are coming up the drive, sir.'

Dupuy nodded to myself, Horst and Kwami. 'We go out on the veranda and make a show of force. If we have to fire, fire over their heads. No one fires until I give the word.'

We all nodded back.

'Follow me.'

We formed a line of four men out on the veranda. Indeed coming up the drive were Kama and dozens of men. When they saw us and our rifles they all stopped.

'Go home!' Dupuy shouted in Lingala.

Kama shouted something back. I do not know what he said, but it certainly sounded defiant. He turned to his men and held his spear in the air and shouted. The men jumped up and down and chanted. Kama called, they responded. He called again, once more they responded.

'Damn it!' Dupuy cursed. 'Kama's telling them his ju-ju will protect them.'

Tshombe said, 'Sir, here they come.'

As Kama and his men walked up the drive Dupuy said, 'Follow my directions precisely. Chamber a round.'

We all put a round up the spout.

'Aim over their heads.' He said. 'Over their heads.'

The four of us took aim.

'On my command...' Kama and his men were within a hundred meters of the veranda. 'Over their heads. Fire!'

A volley of four .30-40 rounds went over Kama and his men. They stopped in their tracks. Many dove to the ground. Some hid behind others.

'Chamber another round,' Dupuy said calmly.

I opened and closed the bolt, a spent cartridge flew out and clanged on the wood floor.

'They are wavering,' Dupuy said. 'Put another round over their heads. On my command...fire!'

The second volley startled them more than the first. A few backed up one ran back down the drive.

Dupuy shouted in Lingala, 'Go away! Go home! Get out of here or we'll kill you!'

Kama stood up and jumped up and down.

'Oh hell,' Dupuy said. 'He's telling them that his ju-ju made the bullets miss.'

'Does he really believe that?' Horst asked.

'I would think so.'

Kwami said, 'Sir, we must fire on them. Here they come.'

'Damn it,' said Dupuy. He stepped forward and took aim. 'Go home, Kama or you die!'

Kama waved his spear in the air and then reared back to throw it.

Dupuy fired a round and hit Kama square in the throat.

This stopped his men in their tracks. They watched as Kama quickly bled out, his heart pumping blood out of the massive hole in his throat and onto his face and chest. He wheezed and gasped and then he was dead. Kama's men looked up at us in confusion and anger.

Next to me Kwami said, 'Sir, you know they will attack, look at them.'

Indeed Kama's men were hopping and shouting and their faces moving from looks of confusion to looks of rage.

'Sir, you know what we must do.'

A few of Kama's men stepped forward, then a few more. As they picked up their pace Dupuy fired, Kwami followed, then Horst and myself. We just kept shooting till we ran out of bullets....

Part II

CHAPTER 1

———

1964

ON THIS MORNING I DO not even have time to see it in the paper before Herr Weder asks, 'Did you hear? Can you believe it?'

'I am sorry, Herr Weder, I do not know to what you refer.'

'MacArthur has died.'

I raise my eyebrows, 'Oh?'

'Can you believe it?'

The man was eighty-four years old. In fact his death is not at all hard to believe. For a moment I pause. MacArthur was just nine years older than myself. Forgive me, but at my age nine years does not seem like such a long time.

Herr Weder talks as he pours my tea but I really do not hear him. Instead my thoughts are of MacArthur. I have long admired the great man. He was a brilliant general during the Great Pacific War and the wise autocrat of Japan. In 1948 the American people, in perhaps their most sensible act ever, elected him President of the United States. Whenever I worry about the SPD reformers in the Bundestag and the press calling for direct democracy, I remind myself that even the Americans managed to elect a wise president like MacArthur.

MacArthur is widely respected in Germany but here the day continues apace. The nation simply has too much vested in our celebrations to let the death of a foreign leader, even a great one, interrupt them. Walking through the Tiergarten one hears bits of conversation about the great man's death. The English take note and nod at the news with a bit of sadness. After all, he led America's defeat of their greatest enemy in the Pacific. The Americans walking the Tiergarten carry on. The death of a great figure in their history will not keep the Americans from their vacation. After a few hours watching them, I hit upon an idea, and by the end of my day I have sold seven MacArthur caricature drawings at fifteen reichsmarks each. Fifteen reichsmarks! Americans...

That night at Otto's the news once more leads off with preparations for the grand celebration. This report takes up the entire first segment of the broadcast. The Kaiser and Chancellor will both be in the reviewing stand for the parade. The parade itself will impress with floats from all over Germany and troop contingents from all corners of the empire. The Luftwaffe's elite Valkyrie aerial acrobatic squadron will make a special flyover. This last bit is an inspired touch. Everyone loves jet planes, and it is rumored the Wilhelm IV's young son is an aircraft enthusiast. The Kaiser will no doubt be pleased.

After the commercial break, the news anchor announces the death of President MacArthur,

'This morning doctors at Walter Reed Army Medical Center in Washington D.C. announced President MacArthur died in his sleep from complications stemming from liver disease. He is survived by his wife, Jean and their son, Arthur. In a life that spanned the 19th and 20th centuries MacArthur graduated from the United States Army Military Academy at West Point, after which he served in America's War with Spain, the Pancho Villa expedition and later the occupation and reconstruction of Mexico.

'MacArthur's greatest military exploits came as commander of the American Central Pacific Area during the Great Pacific War against Japan. Here he liberated the Hawaiian Islands and then oversaw the island-hopping campaign to the Philippines. Under MacArthur's leadership the United States imposed a year-long blockade of Japan, which starved the empire into submission...Viewed controversially by some, the blockade is widely understood to have saved millions if not tens of millions of lives.'

The report went into MacArthur's two terms as president. The anchor quoted a German historian who argued that given his military and political successes, MacArthur was the greatest American since George Washington. I watched and ate my chocolate cake and drank my tea and tried to think of a German ruler to whom MacArthur compared. One is tempted to say Bismarck, given the combination of military and domestic success, but

MacArthur was not a wartime president. Nor did he remake an entire continent as did Bismarck. Let us say he is a close second to the great Bismarck.

When I get home I see Aggie coming down the hall. She walks briskly past me and simply says, 'Good evening' before heading down the stairs. I look down the now empty hall and think, *That Frau is upset!* Just as I get to my door, Bob opens his and looks down the hallway. He's looking for Aggie.

'She is already gone,' I say.

'Damn it,' Bob mutters.

'A fight, eh?' I ask.

Bob shook his head. 'Stupid.'

An argument between two married people is none of my business so I unlock my door and go inside. Then I realize, given current events, how rude I have just been to Bob. He's not only an American citizen but a civil servant in the American government. I go and knock on his door. When he opens I say, 'Please forgive me. I forgot to extend my condolences on the death of your President MacArthur.'

To my surprise Bob nods and laughs, 'That's what we were fighting about.'

'Oh?'

'Would you like to come in?' Bob asks.

We sit down on the Baker's modular American furniture.

'You were fighting over President MacArthur?'

Bob looks at his feet and nods. 'Yeah. I've been at the embassy all day. We've been working on a memorial and prayer service for the president. I just got home.'

'Ah,' I conclude. 'And Aggie is mad that you worked so long.'

'No,' Bob says. 'She is mad that I was working on a memorial for President MacArthur.'

'Really?' I ask.

'She hates MacArthur. Just hates him.'

I ponder this for a moment. It seems astounding to me that someone as intelligent and well-mannered as Aggie could hate a man like MacArthur.

'Why would she hate such a great man?'

Bob holds up his hands. 'I wouldn't know where to start,' he tells me. 'She thinks he was the worst, cruelest president we've ever had.'

This is a woman's opinion. What sane, clear-thinking man would believe such a thing? But a woman, ah yes, of course.

Bob shakes his head again. 'She could explain it to you better than I could. I just don't get it.'

'You are working in your capacity as a member of the embassy are you not?'

Bob nodded. 'I had my problems with MacArthur, who didn't? Ambassador Brundage said we need a great commemoration, so we prepare a great commemoration. It doesn't matter if I disagreed with his handling of the miner's strike, I don't get to make that decision.'

'Does she not understand that?'

'She does,' replied Bob. 'I thought I'd patched things up.'

'You didn't?'

'Not really.'

'Well what angered her then?'

'I admitted to voting for Ford in 1956.' Bob shrugged. 'It was my first election.'

'He was MacArthur's Vice President, was he not?'

'Yeah and he defeated Harriman.'

'And this upset Aggie?'

'Well,' Bob shrugged. 'She wanted Stevenson instead of Harriman for the Democrats. But mostly she just hated Vice President Ford.'

I was mystified at this notion. Three years after he left office, President Ford is already considered a footnote between MacArthur and Kennedy, and his administration is recalled mostly for its general bumbling and mishandling of the Negro issue in America. While Ford dithered over the southern states' refusal to enforce the Supreme Court's judgements on segregation, MacArthur would have sent the army into the schools. That said, I find it hard to imagine that anyone can have strong feelings about the man either way.

'I voted for Kennedy last time. I work for the man. I really don't know what more she wants from me.'

A few minutes later, Aggie returns. She stands in the doorway, still furious. She was about to chastise poor, suffering Bob again, but then she saw me.

'Oh,' she says, somewhat embarrassed. 'I did not know you were here.'

I stand and give a slight bow. 'It is good to see you again, Aggie. I hope all is well.'

'I'm sorry,' she says. 'We were arguing.'

'It is quite alright,' I reply. 'I shall leave you both to it.'

Aggie may be fuming but Bob has had a long day and I can see he simply wants to retire to bed. I walk to the door and say, 'I will still be seeing you tomorrow, will I not?'

Seemingly startled, Aggie says, 'Oh! Yes, of course.'

Later it is evident the two have settled their argument. I just hope they do not wake up Erica.

Aggie and Erica come over the next day before dinner.

'Bob is at the Embassy,' she says. 'The Ambassador is leading a prayer service right now.'

'You do not attend?' I ask.

'No.'

Erica pushes past her mother and runs into my studio.

She runs about looking at my easel, pallet, and paints. Oddly it is the floor canvas that gets her attention.

'Mommy!' Erica says. The canvas is covered in paint, as is Erica. 'It's like yours!'

'Oh my!' I clasp my hands together at the mass of paint Erica has accumulated on the canvas.

To my surprise Aggie retorts, 'It's nothing like my work.'

'I'm sure,' I reply.

'No,' Erica. 'Mommy likes to do funny things with paint.'

I laugh at this, 'Oh I am sure she does more than that. Perhaps I could see some examples?'

'Oh, I'm sure a real artist like you won't think much of my work.'

'I don't think it's up to public scrutiny. Certainly not by a real artist.'

If only she knew some of the no-talent fools I have encountered in my life she would not say such things.

'Oh please don't be that way,' I say. 'Art is art.'

Aggie clearly wants to show me her work but wants to be prodded into doing so, all part of the shyness of a young artist.

She blushes a bit and says, 'Oh, very well.'

Aggie goes back to her apartment. She returns with a thick binder and hands it to me. 'This is something I've put together...'

Being prepared to show one's work is a good first step for a young artist. I open the binder and take a quick flip through the first few prints. Hopefully I hide my disappointment with Aggie. Her work is a mishmash of shapes and colors with no overall purpose. It lacks direction. In short she is an abstract expressionist. Erica is correct, her paint splattering is like her mother's.

'I just love those modern conceptual artists out of New York City.'

I can see that, I merely nod as I flip through the binder.

'Very interesting,' I manage.

Of course Aggie's work is terrible but I would never say that to her. I merely sit quietly and nod as she explains her work to me. She goes on at some length about her brush technique and her choice of colors. Aggie's enthusiasm and genuine love for her craft is obvious but I wish she channeled it into a more relevant form of painting. Her brush technique is not bad, actually. Somehow this talented artist has fallen under the spell of the talentless Expressionists of the New York School. What bores. Erica could paint better than the likes of Pollack or Rothko. She would never be a neo-classicist like myself, she just doesn't have the aesthetic sensibility to appreciate neo-classical art. But there is no reason why she could not be an Impressionist painter adding her touch to a common scene in the vein of a Monet or a Renoir.

It is then that I resolve to try to help Aggie become a better artist.

After my nap I wash and dress and head down to Otto's.

The news is on TV.

The first part of the broadcast notes that President MacArthur's body is lying in-state in the Capitol Rotunda in Washington. I nod in approval. The Americans' Capitol Building encapsulates everything a great building should be, and represents the best in neo-classical design. The Rotunda with its round hall and Greco-Roman statues is most impressive and a fitting space for well-wishers to pay their last respects to the general and president.

After the commercial break the anchor begins again, 'Today in Hamburg a mass protest closed down Hamburg's central square, bringing the work day there to a halt...'

During the last year or so these protests have become increasingly common. I do not like the protests or their purpose. But in truth I cannot help but admire these protestors and their leaders. Here are active, eager and engaged youth taking an interest in their country. When I was that age I was an art school reject, lonely after the death of my mother and wandering listlessly. I tell myself I was a bohemian in the Vienna art scene, but in truth after my art school rejection I did not know what I wanted or what purpose my life served. At least these young people, clad in American clothes and wearing English hair styles know what they want.

The protests are not limited to Hamburg, but a mass movement in all the major cities and university towns. In truth, the young protestors have a point. There was no need for the severity of the Colonial Office's crackdown, as any old Congo hand could have told them. Mobutu and his rebels fought off all efforts by the Colonial Office constabulary. Chancellor Speer dispatched paratroopers and elite jaeger troops to quell the violence. After four years they are still in Congo. More than 50,000 of them rotating in and out of the colony.

The Congo has consumed German politics ever since. The Conservatives are determined to see the conflict through to the end, and given the recent lull in rebel activity they are crowing. The Christian Democrats want a negotiated settlement and argue that with recent German successes, now is the time to ask Mobutu to the negotiating table. The Catholic Center Party wants peace at any price and favors wholesale withdrawal from Congo and eventually the entire empire. They feel the empire is unchristian. I always scoff at that notion. Does the Catholic Center Party not understand what will happen if we just pull out and leave the Africans without our steadying hand? The government and Colonial Office go to tremendous effort to explain this to the German public. Indeed a very large portion of the Tiergarten display is dedicated to the African Pavilion.

The next morning, my interest piqued, I walk over to the African Pavilion and take a look. Immediately I see that this display will be far different than others. Usually in the wake of military conflict the authorities erect great statues to victory and memorials to the dead. Not here. Most of the pavilion is taken up by a display called *The Works of Africa*. I must admit the designers have outdone themselves. They have built a twenty meter high, twenty meter wide three dimensional map of Congo. Thousands upon thousands of tiny plastic trees show the massive woodlands of the colony. The map has scale models of Wilhelmsville and detailed scale re-creations of the massive road cleaved out of the jungle and the railroad running to every corner of Congo. The craftsmanship is remarkable. Further down the walkway is another scale model - this one a massive mineral mine with a cutaway of the various shafts and dozens of tiny models of tractors, diggers, dump trucks, and backhoes. There follows a similar model of the great lumber mill in the deepest part of the jungle near the headwaters of the River Congo.

Behind me an accented voice says, 'Guten tag, mein Herr.'

I turn around. Standing before me are a young African man and woman. Both are tall and healthy looking with the darkest skin that positively gleams in the sun. They are dressed in slacks and button-down shirts, and appear to be as well made and kempt as any young German couple. Curiously, their hair is most un-African, straight and combed over in the western style.

'Guten tag,' I reply.

The young woman says, 'I am Josephine.'

The young man adds, 'I am Lionel. May we tell you about our nation?'

So they are calling it a nation, I think to myself. 'I would love to hear about it,' I reply, curious as to what this pair will say.

It turns out they are from Goma a small town in the east near Lake Wilhelm. They were educated by Catholic nuns and then attended school in Germany. Some colonial office functionary no doubt found these two and plucked them out of the Congo thinking they would be a great part of the Congo Expedition.

'Do you speak Lingala?' I ask.

Lionel looks most surprised. How could an old German man know about one of Congo's languages? 'Nein,' he replies. 'We are both Swahili speakers.'

Josephine asks, 'Do you know our country?'

'Yes, I visited Congo once.'

'Really, when?' Josephine asked.

'A long time ago. Long before you were born.'

'How wonderful,' Lionel says.

Josephine asked, 'What do you think of our homeland?'

Of course I avoid mentioning the unpleasant parts so I merely give them impressions of the place, the greenery, the raw power of the River Congo.

When finished, I nod and say, 'Well, I shall not keep you from your work. Good day.'

'Good day!' the two enthusiastically reply.

One can train anybody, I suppose.

I walk on until I find what I am looking for. The Congo Memorial. This solemn placard commemorates the more than 10,000 German soldiers killed in Congo over the last five years. The Memorial is really no memorial at all, but a large information placard packed with maps and photographs. The photographs are interesting for what they do not show. I see no photographs of troops storming trenches, or artillery batteries hammering enemy positions. Instead, the panel shows German soldiers giving medical attention to Congolese civilians, German heavy bulldozers pushing earth around for a new dam, an excavator digging a new well. Most of the work is being done by Congolese. Always German officers command but are not pictured in a domineering way. Rather they almost look like big brothers. One German officer, directing a gang of Congolese railroad workers even wears a scraggly beard, cleverly showing that he has spent much time in the Congo and he's 'gone native' as the English would say.

I move on to a sub panel titled, 'The Emerging Congolese Army'. Here is a quick description of the General Staff's efforts to train and build a native army. There is one photograph of a company of native troops all standing at attention. Another shows native soldiers clad in German issue jungle camouflage and jungle hat. They kneel before a standing German officer distinguishable by the black grease smeared over his milky white face. Another photo shows a pair of Congolese soldiers in the field lying in a patch of tall grass, their rifles at the ready and pointed at an off-picture enemy.

Off to the side of the photographic display a tall, fit-looking man in light gray uniform sees me examining the picture. He wears captain's bars and his face holds the weariness of a combat veteran. He has the eyes of an old man but I doubt he is older than 25. He greets me most politely.

'Do you have any questions, mein Herr?'

'Oh....I was just looking,' I reply. 'Tell me, have you served in Congo?'

'Oh yes,' he says. 'Twice. Once in command of a jaeger platoon, once in command of a company.'

'Will you be heading back?'

'Hopefully no.'

'But we only follow orders from the General Staff, eh?' I gently nudge him in the ribs.

'Ah, a veteran yourself, mein Herr?'

'Ja, 16th Bavarian Reserve Infantry Regiment.' I click my heels and nod.

'A pleasure, mein Herr.' We shake hands. 'I am Captain Gerhardt Wilhelm. At your service, mein Herr.'

I dismiss Captain Wilhelm's formality.

I point to the photographic display. 'This is not the kind of war I fought,' I say. 'We just marched and fought. Marched and fought. We never thought about the civilians. Just find the enemy and engage.'

Wilhelm nodded. 'I am almost envious. All we do is think about Congolese.'

'In what way?' I ask.

'How to get them on our side.'

'Hence all of your good deeds in Congo.'

'You catch on, mein Herr.'

I retell my own tale of intrigue and violence in Congo. Wilhelm says. 'Ah, ju-ju men. We work very hard to discredit them.'

'Does it work?'

'Sometimes.'

I laugh. 'Many say the troublemakers are stoked by Russian agitators.'

Wilhelm scoffed at the idea. 'A Russian could not make heads or tail of Congo.'

'I do not think so either,' I said, thinking of my own time fighting them in the Great War.

'No, the trouble comes from locals,' Wilhelm said, 'Perhaps with some help from the French.'

We both laughed at that. French efforts at intrigue in Africa are legendary for their perfidy and spectacular failure. In the 1940s a French planter tried to foment a revolution in the eastern Congo provinces around Kigali only to be arrested by Colonial police. Gallut insisted he had been working with the French Secret Police. Paris denied the accusation, of course, but the Colonial Office always wondered where M. Gallut got two thousand French-made bolt action rifles. The French never learned, assuming that because Congo was French speaking that the people there were part of 'L'isle de France' and susceptible to French intrigue. Paris was forever trying to avenge their defeat in the Great War, even fifty years later.

Some British tourists were perusing the Congo display. Captain Wilhelm said, 'If you will excuse me, mein Herr.'

'Of course.'

'It was a pleasure.'

He nods and walks over to the English tourists. Of course, with their great empire, the English had more than their share of revolutions with which to deal - most recently the Zionist terrorists in Palestine, a gang of messianic mad-men who thought god ordained Palestine to the Jews. For a decade the English SAS had been chasing them down.

Not all dissent within the British Empire is violent or ended with violent means. Parliament placated India by granting the sub-continent Dominion status. Recently there is even talk of appointing Mr. Nehru, head of the Indian National Congress, Governor General of all India. Given the press of history and the ambitions of India, I suspect this is inevitable.

CHAPTER 2

———

BEFORE I CAN EVEN PUT my bag down I hear a tiny but furious and insistent knock on the door. I open it to see Erica standing there. She holds a piece of paper aloft and says, 'I painted you a painting!'

'I see!' I say enthusiastically.

Erica thrusts the paper in my hand. It is a painting of me. I must say the child has worked quite hard, and even captured the sense of me, especially my long, thin face and mustache. Awkwardly she has caricatured my nose, a facial feature about which I have always been sensitive.

'Well, thank you very much my dear,' I say.

Aggie comes out into the hallway.

'Erica, don't bother him,' she says. Aggie looks at me. 'I'm sorry.'

'No, it is alright. Erica has drawn me a very nice picture.'

'Can we work on German?' Erica asked.

I say, 'Sprechen sie Deutsch?'

Erica laughs and repeats.

'Erica!' Aggie comes over and takes Erica by the arm. 'So sorry.'

I laugh.

'You see, she is already so excited because our TV is coming today.'

'Oh, of course.'

'You would not happen to know what channel children's programs are on, would you?'

'Sorry, I do not even own a TV.'

'Oh.'

'But I will ask.'

'I appreciate it.'

Not much later, the movers from the previous day arrive. The Smart and Dumb ones come up the stairs. The Smart One measures the width of the stairway and then the hallway.

'You already did that,' the Dumb One says.

'Just being thorough.'

I remember the man's fresh battle scar. He learned that kind of attention to detail in the Wehrmacht for certain.

The Smart One sees me and says, 'We meet again, mein Herr.'

'There is no need for such formality.' I introduce myself.

'Ja, I am Karl Wulfe. This is my brother Peter.'

Peter nods, 'Hello.'

Karl says to his brother, 'Give the man one of our business cards.'

Peter produces a white business card from his shirt pocket and hands it to me.

Jaeger-Wulfe Moving, says the card.

'Jaeger?' I ask.

Karl Wulfe points to the scar across his arm. 'I was in the jaegers for two years.' He points to the jaeger logo on the card, an idealized 18th century soldier holding a musket and wearing a peaked hat.

'I see,' I say. 'Did you serve in the Congo, then?'

'That is where I received this scar.'

I extend my hand again. 'Sixteenth Bavarian Reserve Infantry Regiment.'

'Ah!' He says. 'A fellow soldat.'

'Some time ago, I am afraid.'

'Eastern Front?'

I nod.

'Ja,' Karl says. 'I got this scar at Bethmann-Hollwegville three years ago. One of Mobutu's little fuzzy-wuzzy terrorists tried to shoot me at point blank range. But none of them can shoot. He only grazed me.'

Karl patted his scar almost affectionately.

'I got him, though. And many of his friends.'

'I gather those were the dark days.'

'You say dark days as if they have passed,' Karl says.

'They have not?'

Karl shakes his head. 'If you believe the television. My comrades still there say something different. In fact….'

'Hey,' Peter says, 'Can we please deliver this television?'

Karl uttered some curses against his brother and excused himself.

The two strongmen returned with a large wooden crate. Their muscles stress and their faces appear strained and covered with sweat. The crate fit up the stairway and into the hall but not through the door, so Karl and Peter pry open the crate and take the television out. Fortunately, the always convenience-minded Americans built the television with rollers. Aggie thanks the brothers and tips them.

I wave to Karl and say, 'Good luck to you now.'

'Oh, we will see you in a few days, mein Herr.'

'What did I say,' I replied. 'There is no need for such formality.'

'Apologies, mein Herr, but if my drill sergeant heard I was not properly addressing an old veteran he would give me the thrashing of a lifetime.'

I nod and smile at Karl. This young combat veteran was the epitome of youthful respect, so unlike the young people on the television today.

'We have more items to deliver,' Karl says.

'Ja,' Peter agrees.

'So see you in a few days.'

I wave.

Erica very excitedly calls me into the Bakers' apartment to see the family television. She hops up and down as I walk into the apartment, takes my hand and leads me right over to the contraption. Most German families have televisions now, but these are usually small and fit into a corner where they are kept until a program comes on. This TV is not like that. Covered in wood paneling with large cabinets on either side of the screen, this television is a piece of furniture intended to dominate the room in which it is placed. Erica is most enthusiastic and shows off the TV to me.

'Look!' Erica says.

She pulls back a top panel. 'Look inside.'

I peer inside as instructed. 'Oh my,' I say. Here is a radio console.

She walks to the other side of the television and pulls back another panel. 'This is even neater!'

On the other side is a record player.

'I can't wait to play my records for you!' Erica says.

'Neither can I,' I say.

Erica smiles and claps some more.

'Perhaps later?' I ask, feeling the cumulative effects of the day wear on me.

That evening Otto gives me a list of several children's programs.

The next morning, I find a piece of paper taped to my door. I open and see a child's writing. Erica has invited me to come over this afternoon and watch television with her. She has drawn a picture of the two of us holding hands.

I walk down to Weder's café. Already humidity is in the air. I pick up a newspaper and order my tea. I sit and read the headline.

TUMULT IN CONGO

Riots in interior town of Kindu.

Colonial Branch Office Burned

Kindu, Congo: Yesterday terrorists loyal to Mobutu attacked Colonial offices in the interior provincial town of Kindu, killing the local prefect and burning the office to the ground. In addition, police dispatched to help the colonial officer came under small arms fire and had to turn back. At least one was killed.

Herr Weder brings me a cup of tea and says, 'Can you believe that? Those jungle fuzzies!'

Even with the recent violence against white farmers, a brazen attack on a colonial prefecture comes as a surprise. I read on looking for the good news but none is forthcoming, at least not if one knows how to read a newspaper. The writers and editors of *Der Spiegel* would never lie, of course, not even when faced with the most enormous government pressure. But they will dance around and avoid information and write in a certain way to indicate things the government does not like. For example, this article does not say that the fighting has ended, only that German forces are securing the nation. The article does not say that the perpetrators have been apprehended, only that the police were looking for them. Nor does it mention enemy casualties. Of course there are none. Everything we really need to know is between the lines. In essence, the crisis within Kindu is ongoing.

'We should really let them have it!'

I bite my tongue. Having been on the receiving end of an enemy rifle, I do not relish the idea of sending young men into harm's way, at least not without good reason. And having killed Africans in my own Congo foray, I'd like not to see it happen again. In my old age I have simply come to abhor violence. It is different for Herr Weder. Like all German men, he did performed three years' military service. He was an infantrymen in the 1940's stationed in Poland with Das Vistula Korps. But he was a peacetime soldier and has never seen the kind of carnage I witnessed in the 16th Bavarian Reserve Infantry Regiment.

News of the parade a few days hence consumes the rest of *Der Spiegel's* front page. I read on with interest.

When I return to my building, Karl and Peter are coming out of the Bakers' apartment. Karl is wiping his hands and says, 'That is the last of it.'

Behind him Peter says, 'These Americans.'

'Careful,' I laugh. 'They are learning German.'

'Oh, hello,' Karl says.

'Ja, ja, guten tag, mein Herr.' Karl sees the newspaper tucked under my arm. 'What a mess.'

'I am afraid so.'

'We worked very hard to clean up that place.'

'You were in Kindu?'

'Ja, I was in Kindu.'

I hold up the newspaper and point at the map.

'Ja, that is it.'

'The paper says there is a lot of trouble there.'

'Well outside in the bush the natives could be a handful.'

I hold the paper up, 'This says the trouble is in Kindu proper.'

'Really?' Karl asked. 'May I?'

He takes the paper and reads. 'I recognize this building. And now Mobutu's men have torched it.' Karl shakes his head. 'Unbelievable. Why I remember...' Karl stopped himself.

'Is there something wrong?'

'You probably do not want to hear the reminiscences of a veteran.'

Behind Karl his own brother says, 'Ja, I know I am sick of hearing about Congo.'

Karl curses at his brother, 'Shut up you Luftwaffe, rear echelon paper clip ranger.'

'Someone had to file the paper work,' Peter replies. He points to Karl and says, 'He cannot shut up about his time in Congo.'

I nod my head, not at what the oafish Peter is saying, but in sympathy with Karl. I place a paternalistic hand on his shoulder. 'Young man, you are welcome to tell me all about your time in Congo.'

'Really?' he replies.

'In fact, I think you might make an interesting character study.'

Peter says, 'Watch it Karl, I bet he is one of those new age artists.'

Karl reaches out a strong hand and slaps his brother across the back of the head. 'Shut up.' He says. 'He is a combat veteran like me.'

One should never get between two quarreling brothers, so I say nothing.

'Ja, I would be happy to come by.'

'Fag,' Peter says. 'I knew it.'

Karl glares at his brother. 'My fiancée would probably enjoy a sketch of me.'

'Ja, he feels he needs to impress her. I said she already has the ring so he can relax.'

Without taking his eyes from me, Karl reaches out and punches his brother in the arm. He lands a direct hit which sends Peter reeling and rubbing his arm.

'Wonderful, then,' I reply. 'Shall you come at seven?'

'Ja, of course.' Karl bows and nods slightly. 'I shall see you tomorrow then.'

The brothers leave. Though Karl clearly wants to impress this fiancée of his I suspect that part of him simply wants to help an old man who is a veteran himself. So be it. I am too old to worry about people seeing me as a charity case.

After Karl and Peter leave, Aggie pops out into the corridor. 'Hello!' Aggie declares in her typically enthusiastic American style. 'You got our note?'

'Ja,' I nod.

'So you will be coming over, then.'

I bow and say, 'I would love to.'

'Wonderful, we'll have dinner.' I do not even have a chance to start my objection to Aggie going to any trouble for me. 'And I won't take no for an answer!'

I meekly say, 'I would not dream of saying no.'

'Oh good.' Aggie replies. 'Erica is so excited about having you over.'

'I look forward to it,' I say. Thinking of my afternoon shower and nap I say, 'If you will excuse me.'

After my nap and shower I dress in coat and tie and knock on the Bakers' door. Erica opens the door and enthusiastically invites me. Bob comes to the door clad in trousers and an open collared shirt. These informal Americans. Erica is wearing her best dress, I see. She takes my hand and walks me over to the couch by the television.

'Erica we are not having a guest over to just plop him down in front of the TV.'

'But mom, I want to show him my new favorite show!'

'I am sure he already knows about German children's cartoons and doesn't want to watch them, young lady. Help me set the table.'

Erica reluctantly follows her mother.

I smell dinner coming from the kitchen, something meaty to be sure, and I am wondering how to politely decline. Bob says, 'Can I get you something to drink? Beer? I have a six pack of American beer.'

Out of curiosity I agree to one. Bob hands me a glass bottle labelled *Miller*. The beer, I hesitate to call it, is a kind of light brown, almost yellow, and thin. Though I am not much of a beer drinker, one swig of this Miller and I know I will not be able to finish the thin gruel. Have the Americans no aesthetic taste?

'How is the American embassy?' I ask, trying to make small talk.

'Getting back to normal now that the vigil is over.'

'Ah, good.'

'Well, they're bringing me up to speed on things here.'

'Ah.'

'And a tutor spends two hours a day teaching me German.' Bob Baker says in German, 'I am coming along.'

I nod. Indeed he is getting better, his accent has become ever so slightly more German, Berliner of course.

'We were working on the Great War celebration. But with this latest outbreak of violence in Congo we dropped everything and put together a report.'

'Really?'

'The Ambassador has a telephone call with Secretary Rusk tomorrow.'

'I suppose the Kennedy government wants to know about this latest act in Congo.'

'Yes, I have to say State is very concerned.'

Aggie chimes in. 'I just think it's awful what the German government is doing.'

Bob Baker looks askance at his wife, though I cannot tell if he is upset that she is opining about politics at all or because she is criticizing the government with me at the table.

Bob attempts to steer the conversation back to the minutiae of his work day.

'Awww...' Erica says. 'I hate it when daddy talks about work.'

Bob continues. 'Well I can tell you State views civil rights in Congo as part and parcel with civil rights in the United States.

'I certainly hope so,' Aggie adds.

Being a polite guest I say nothing about the irony of a nation that has a huge legal infrastructure for suppressing Negroes criticizing Germany for possessing colonies in Africa.

Aggie points to me and says, 'He's been there, you know.'

I blush. 'Yes, a long time ago.'

'It seems little has changed,' Aggie says bitterly.

As I understand the situation in Africa, this is true. Forty years after my tour of Congo, the colony is still run by a small administration that in truth only rules the big cities and forays out into the country side only as needed.

'Well,' Bob asked, 'what would you do?'

I try to fend off the question, after all I am no colonial office administrator, but Bob insists. 'Come now. You have been on scene, as we say. You must know something about running the place.'

I shrug and take a bite of broccoli to give me time to collect my thoughts. 'Well, look what the British have achieved in India,' I offer. 'The nation is run by Indians is it not?'

'Yes, but for the British,' Aggie says.

'True, I suppose. But the nation is part of the empire. It is one of their dominions on par with Canada and Australia is it not?' I ask Bob, being a diplomat.

'You know, he's right,' Bob says to Aggie. 'And they are doing the same thing with their African colonies. Building an indigenous governing class to run the place in their name.'

Aggie pushes her food around her plate and says, 'I just think people have the right to self-determination.'

I believe leaving the African to his own devices is madness, but do not say so. This will no doubt provoke Aggie and we are having a pleasant enough dinner. Knowing his wife's passions, Bob, as any good husband should, changes the subject.

We finish dinner. I offer to help clean up but Erica insists upon showing me the record player in the television console. She plays me one her mother's records by those mop-topped young English miscreants. Erica dances and bops around to the song and as I listen to their musicianship, I can see why Erica likes them so much. 'Love, love me do' might as well be a children's song. It is one thing for English and especially American children to enjoy this music, but I am dismayed that the youth of Germany is also consuming this tripe.

A second song begins, but mercifully Aggie emerges from the kitchen and invites me to sit on the couch.

We sit down and watch a teledrama.

'Oh,' Aggie, says, 'I found this program last night.'

She gets up and walks over to the television, leans down and changes the channel. The piece of furniture looks comically large next to Aggie, and I marvel at the ability of the Americans to make anything larger than necessary.

A quick news promo comes on about plans for the parade in two days. We see a commercial for a Volkswagen, then the screen fades. First we hear minimalist, futuristic sounding music. Then the picture appears and we see a backdrop of a nighttime sky, positively brimming with stars. Erica points and 'oooohs' at the TV. Then large block letters assault the screen coming from the darkness at the viewer one by one and then receding to the background until they spell, HEISENBERG. Ah, of course.

'Heisenberg,' I say. 'I have seen this program on occasion.'

The screen fades again and the space backdrop falls behind a television studio containing a coffee table and three chairs. Werner Heisenberg walks onto the set, dapper in a suit and black horn-rimmed glasses. He sits in the chair on the far left and begins.

'Good evening and welcome to *Heisenberg*. Today joining me is…

'Ugh…' Erica exclaims. 'This is so boring mommy!'

'Shh!' Aggie says.

Bob offers, 'Come, Erica. Let's go play.'

'Ok!' Erica says rather enthusiastically. She looks to me and says, 'Do you want to come play?'

Aggie chimes in, 'Oh, leave him alone.'

I am grateful as my seventy-five-year-old frame will not easily get down on the floor or back up. I add, 'Later we can paint.'

'Yay!' Erica says.

'It's good for Erica to spend a little time with her dad,' Aggie says. 'To be honest, I could use the break.'

I nod sympathetically, though I can only imagine as I have children of my own.

Heisenberg introduces his guest.

Aggie says 'I think he is so interesting. You know, a few years ago he came to America on a book tour.'

I did not know that.

'Yes he was promoting that book about Physics…,' Aggie searched for the name. 'Ah, *The Atom Possible.*'

Now that she mentioned it, I had heard of Heisenberg's book.

'He says it is possible to split the atom.'

'Oh yes,' I recalled I had heard that theory, splitting the atom would release a massive amount of energy. 'Would that not be dangerous? The release of such massive amounts of energy?'

'It could be used for peaceful purposes, energy and such.'

Clearly Aggie is smitten by the idea and she goes on a bit. So as not to be rude, I feign interest. In truth, science has never interested me, even now with a celebrity physicist on the television.

When the show is over it is time for me to retreat to my studio. As I head toward the door I say, 'Oh, Aggie, I had almost forgotten. Your mover is coming by my apartment tomorrow night for a sitting.'

I explain the conversation Karl and I had earlier.

She raises an eyebrow. 'Oh how nice.'

'Would you like to join us?'

'And sketch too?'

'Ja, of course. You are an artist, are you not?'

Aggie blushes a bit, clearly flattered that an old artist considers her as an artist worthy of working with him.

'Well, I…' She looks at Erica.

'Can I come, too?'

'No sweetie, you'll be in bed.' Aggie looks to Bob.

Bob encourages his wife. 'Sure, go on, honey, I can get Erica to bed.' Bob Baker looks to their daughter. 'It can be a special Erica -Daddy night.'

Erica claps her hands. 'Yay!'

'It is settled,' I say. 'Karl is going to come by about eight.'

Bob says, 'Well, this sounds like it will be a lot of fun.'

Karl arrived at my apartment at seven PM. He wore street clothes, but over his shoulder hung two uniforms.

'I brought my combat fatigues and my dress uniform.'

'Wonderful,' I say. I invite him in. He sees Aggie sitting in my studio.

'Oh,' he says. 'Hello, Mrs. Baker.'

'I hope you do not mind, but I thought Aggie might like to sketch you as well.'

'Sure. It is fine with me. Which uniform would you like first?'

'Why not your dress uniform?' I suggest.

Karl excuses himself to change in the bedroom. He emerges in his uniform - gray blazer with white lapels and epaulettes, white shirt, black tie and pants. Atop his head rests a red beret with silver parachute pin, marking Karl as a member of the elite jaegers. Across his chest are a row and a half of campaign ribbons. Below those are pinned a marksmanship badge and an airborne school badge. Karl is an accomplished soldier.

'So what would you like me to do?' Karl asked.

'I would say just sit in the chair and we shall sketch.' I look at Aggie, 'Ja?'

'Yep.'

Karl takes a seat and we each do a sketch of him. Much to my relief Aggie sketches Karl as he is, no abstraction, no artistic license. She simply produces a competent and honest work of Karl posing in his uniform.

'Now stand,' I say.

We sketch again. This time Aggie puts a bit of rhetorical flourish in her work. In Aggie's interpretation, Karl seems to be looking forward to what lies ahead. I must say I enjoy what she has sketched out.

'Now would you mind changing into your combat fatigues?'

'No problem at all,' Karl says.

These are a light gray overlaid with green, brown and dark yellow patches.

'Should I sit?'

'If you like.'

Karl sits in the chair and crosses his legs. We compose quick sketches of him. Again, Aggie adds a bit of flourish, using dark lines forward to imply bad tidings ahead. This bit of license could be taken as a political statement I suppose, but it is also a simple statement of fact. Karl is after all wearing combat fatigues.

'You know what?' Aggie says, 'I'd like to sketch your medals, if you don't mind.'

'Nein, I do not mind.'

Karl starts to take his campaign ribbons off but Aggie says, 'No, no. Leave them on your chest like that.'

'Very well,' Karl says.

Aggie sits across from Karl and quickly sketches out his campaign and school ribbons. With pencils she colors her sketched medals to match those on Karl's chest. When finished she turns her sketchbook around and shows it to Karl. 'What do you think?' she asks.

'Ja, good,' Karl nods.

'Now what do all these mean?'

Karl points to a black and red ribbon, 'This one is for the first Congo Campaign, this yellow and black one is for Operation Macher.'

'Operation Macher?' I ask.

'A big sweep, clear and hold effort north of Goma,' he says. 'We really socked Mobutu too.' He resumes describing the campaign ribbons, 'This maroon and black one is for the second Congo Campaign...'

'You went back?' Aggie asks.

'Ja, two tours. This yellow and red ribbon is for Operation Fenster...'

'Oh, I remember that one on the news,' I say. 'That was your jaeger battalion?'

'Ja.'

Indeed two years ago Operation Fenster was something of a sensation. One Jaeger battalion helicoptered directly into a rebel-held village while another parachuted behind the village to cut off the rebels' escape. The ensuing action was more of massacre than a battle.

'Ja,' Karl saiys. 'I led a machinegun squad that jumped down behind the rebels. We set up our guns and slaughtered them as they fled the village.'

'That's horrible,' Aggie saiys.

'That is war, Frau Baker,' says Karl. 'They could have surrendered.'

Karl closes his eyes for just a moment, and I could tell he was back in Operation Fenster seeing the Mobutu men fleeing before the oncoming jaeger helicopters only to be cut down by Karl and his machineguns.

'They said you killed a thousand of them.'

'Ja,' Karl replied. 'The ground before us was carpeted with bodies.'

Aggie opened her sketch book to a fresh page. 'Tell me more about it,' she says.

'We just kept firing.' Karl says. 'At first a long line of trucks and jeeps came out of the town. They were speeding down that road, far too quickly. The reports said we caused a road jam, but in truth the rebels did it to themselves. One truck turned over, then a jeep flipped. You could hear the Africans screaming as their vehicle went into the air.'

'Oh my,' Aggie says as she sketches away.

'I told my men to hold their fire while all this was happening. Behind them on the other end of the village we heard and saw the choppers, they fired at everything they saw. That's why the Mobutu men just kept coming. When the road was all jammed up they just came out of town on foot. We let them come out.'

'Why?' Aggie asks.

'A few months earlier we cleared out Kindu. It was house-to-house fighting, hand grenades. When they wouldn't give up we gave them the flame throwers. Have you ever heard the sound of a man screaming because he is covered in burning napalm?'

Aggie shook her head.

'So we let them come out of town. That's when we opened fire. We must have had a dozen MGs forward by then. I swear it was like watching volley fire from one of those movies about the 1871 War. A hundred Mobutu men must have dropped in the first second, and another hundred after that. I can still see the bullets slamming into their bodies. A red mist seemed to hang in the air, you know that heavy Congo air?'

I nod.

You could actually see it settling on their faces. All around them, trucks and jeeps exploded as we hit their fuel tanks. But they just kept coming out of the town like African termites because B Company was coming up behind them. They brought their flamethrowers. And when it was all over the vehicles were in flames and the ground before us….Half of them were dead. Half of them were alive. And they let us know it. It looked like snakes. A carpet of writhing, squirming, moaning, crying, screaming snakes.'

Then Karl laughs, first a chuckle then a long body-convulsing guffaw that left tears in his eyes.

'What is so funny?' Aggie asks.

'You are all horrified, but that is not even the worst part.'

I say, 'I think I know where you are going with this.'

'We could not help the wounded.'

'Why not?' Aggie demands.

'Because the ju-ju men tell them that killing a white man will heal their wounds.'

'That is ridiculous,' Aggie says.

'It is true,' Karl replies. 'I once saw a wounded rebel knife one of our medics in the gut as he tended to his wounds. They both died, let me tell you.' Karl goes on. 'We did not want to sit there and listen to the wounded. And we were not going to wade into that corpse pile to shoot them individually.'

Karl laughs again.

'So you know what we did?'

Aggie says nothing.

'We called in the mortars. Those frag shells took care of them. Exploded above the field and tore them to bits. You could see the slime of their bodies bouncing off the ground and back into the air.'

He chuckled one last time.

'That shut them the hell up, I can tell you that. When the barrage was finished I sat back, ate a ration and had a smoke.'

Aggie buried her head in her sketch. I watched Karl very closely. He did not seem upset, in fact he seemed almost relieved.

'Thank you for sharing that with us,' I say.

Karl shrugged. 'I never told anyone that before. Except Peter.'

'Oh dear,' I say.

'Ja, he just asked why I would feel bad about seeing a bunch of jungle-fuzzies get killed.'

'He is a fool.'

'Ja,' says Karl. 'But he is my brother.'

Aggie turned her sketch pad around. 'Is this what it looked like?'

She shows a sketch of a field strewn with bodies.

'In a sense, yes, as long as that is before we called in the mortars.'

'What did it look like after?'

Karl shook his head, 'Just a field of slime. Goop. Sometimes you'd see a watch or maybe a boot.'

'Ah,' Aggie says. 'So after that the natives were pretty pissed, I guess.'

I think Karl was going to laugh again, but no. His face becomes serious. 'Are you kidding? We posted photos of the massacre all over Kindu. And the local tribes? Well we gave them a personal tour of the battlefield. After that we had no trouble in Kindu or the surrounding area.'

'I guess they were scared,' says Aggie.

Now Karl laughs. He looks at me but points to Aggie. 'Does this American understand anything about the African mind?'

'What is that supposed to mean?' Aggie asks.

Karl does not answer. Instead he says, 'The natives were not scared. They looked at the battlefield, I really should not call it that, we fought no battle… they looked at the field and decided we were the strongest tribe.'

Having seen this on Dupuy's plantation all those years ago, I nod.

'We never had any trouble after that. In fact, with some of the more primitive tribes, we used our ju-ju in the massacre. Our ju-ju was stronger than any of their ju-ju,' Karl snickered. 'I suppose in a way that's true.'

'That's cruel,' says Aggie.

'It kept the peace,' Karl says. 'Besides…'

Agie holds up her hand. 'I know what you are going to say,' Aggie replies. 'That I've no right to criticize Germany in the Congo when America treats its Negroes so horribly. Well, we are trying to pass civil rights legislation and…'

'I was not going to say you treat your Negroes as horribly as we do.'

'Oh.'

'You do not massacre them as we have, do you?'

Aggie really has nothing to say to that.

CHAPTER 3

———

THE DAY BEFORE THE GRAND Review, I leave my apartment and find a child's drawing taped to my door. It is Erica's and it portrays the three of us attending tomorrow's Grand Review. It is curious to see myself as drawn by Erica. I am of average height, but skinny. There, again, is my mustache and Erica has taken the time to exaggerate my nose. At this I laugh.

The Bakers' apartment door flies open. There stands Erica.

'Can you come? Can you come?' she asks.

Aggie appears behind her daughter and says to me. 'I'm sorry, she's over-eager and excited.'

I nod. 'Why, it would be my pleasure to attend the Grand Review with you, Frau Erica.'

Erica claps her hands, jumps up and down and shouts, 'Yay!'

'Sorry,' Aggie smiles. 'Bob's working at the embassy all day…'

'Not at all. Shall we say nine o'clock?'

'Nine!' Erica shouts. 'Nine, Mom. He said nein, Mom. Nine!'

I am just returning to my apartment when the phone rings. It is Otto.

'The television is live-broadcasting MacArthur's funeral and I thought you would enjoy watching.'

'What time?' I ask.

'In…thirty seven minutes.'

I think for a moment. It is time for my regular nap, but how often does one get to view a funeral such as this? I tell Otto I will be down right away.

When I get to his bar, I see that a few of those young people from the other day are sitting at what has become their regular table. They see me and raise their beer glasses. I nod in return and take my seat at the bar. Otto has turned the TV to the bar and two news anchors gab among each other about President MacArthur's legacy. Behind them is an image of Washington, DC beneath a cloudy sky.

I did not think the Americans were capable of the funeral display of the type I am watching. The ceremony is most un-American, with dignity and class. The president's casket is carried in a hearse drawn by four black horses and led by one white stallion. Before the casket walk Mrs. MacArthur and their son, both in black, of course. President Kennedy has assigned his younger brother, John, the Senator from Massachusetts to escort the bereaved. A great phalanx of generals, most of whom served under MacArthur, follow the caisson. The three service chiefs lead the way. There's Admiral McCain, Naval Chief of Staff, and General Westmoreland, Army Chief. The streets are lined with well-wishers and those otherwise lining up to pay their respects. Washington being a humid city, it rains on this August day.

The caisson brings the casket to Arlington Cemetery, where President Kennedy awaits. The choice of pall bearer is interesting. Young Arthur leads them, of course. There follow two generals, both of whom were close aides and another whom I do not recognize. He looks to be about the same age as MacArthur, tall and trim with white hair that used to be blonde. He has a long forehead and even in old age, one sees a youthful gleam about him. Finally one of the anchors tells us that this is a retired army general who used to be an aide to MacArthur in Washington and later the Philippines.

When the pallbearers put the casket in place, the president gives a quick and glowing eulogy. When he is finished, a Marine bugler plays taps and then members of the 3rd Regiment, the Old Guard, fire a 21-gun salute into the air. Finally, as Mrs. and Arthur MacArthur look on, the coffin is lowered into the grave.

That night Otto's is actually quite full, and I see many people I do not recognize. I also hear many accents, some the familiar and comforting Bavarian, a few Rhinelanders. Otto has kept my table open. I sit there and he brings me a piece of cake.

'This is new,' he says. I take a bite. It is rich and I eat it quickly.

'Who are all these people?' I ask.

'Tourists!' Otto relies, happy at the increased business. 'For the parade.'

'Here?' I reply.

'It seems I am listed in a Berlin tourist guide and recommended for my old world feel.'

'A touch of the old Germany for the tourists, I imagine.'

Otto smiles.

The television news leads with a long piece about the parade plans. The anchor breathlessly reports about the military marching, the politicos in attendance and of course the Kaiser's plans. He will be in the parade, we are told. In fact, he will lead it before taking his seat at the front of the grand dais. They then go to a live report from the dais, still under construction. A serious-looking news reporter tells us that the Kaiser will be accompanied by most of the imperial family. As well, here will be seated important foreign dignitaries. The ambassadors of France and Russia were invited to attend but declined. The British ambassador will be attending, in place of Queen Elizabeth. The American ambassador will be in attendance as well, and I wonder how much Bob will be involved.

From there the news anchor tells us that all is quiet in Congo. I find this troubling. If anything, this Mobutu person would want to make a nuisance of himself on the eve of Victory Week.

I finish my cake and head home.

The next day, when I go over to the Bakers' apartment, Aggie is packing a cooler for the parade. She puts several canteens inside, sandwiches and American snacks.

'Will you really need all that?'

'We intend to be there all day,' Aggie says.

'Standing in the summer sun?'

She points to a stack of lawn chairs. 'We have chairs.'

Americans, I shake my head. Their comforts come with them wherever they go.

'You must bring your sketch book.'

'Why?' Aggie asked.

'I want to see you draw. I want to see you do something realistic.'

Aggie nods and raises an eyebrow 'OK.'

'There will be much military in attendance. This will provide an excellent opportunity for you.'

Aggie, Erica and I get a good spot near the Brandenburg Gate. Already the sidewalks are filling with people. Berlin police have set up barriers to keep people off the circle. The day is cloudy and humid. I am glad for the clouds as they give this old man relief from the sun. Gradually the sidewalk fills up until we are crowded on both sides and pressed by people. It seems to my eye that at least half the spectators are foreigners. The Americans are easily identifiable by their loud clothes, especially those horrible baseball caps of theirs.

Promptly at nine o'clock, a 21-gun salute announces the beginning of the parade. A phalanx of mounted policemen ride down the Tiergarten, indicating the parade start and ensuring the route is clear. They are followed by the mayor of Berlin's ceremonial guard of motorcycle police, their sirens blaring. The mayor rides in an open-topped Mercedes limousine which will take him to the Brandenburg Gate pavilion. The mayor's grandstanding is off-putting. No one is here to see him. Finally when the mayor's caravan passes, the real attractions begin. First comes a company from the elite Prussian Guards Division. They are splendid in dress uniforms, knee boots polished, helmets gleaming, rifles at the shoulder. Other companies pass, one from the elite paratroopers brigade, another from the Kriegsmarine and I am proud to see a representative company from the 1st Bavarian Mountaineers.

There follow colonial contingents from across the empire, young, strong black men clad in German tropical uniforms but wearing exotic headgear. The contingent from Congo leads the procession. First comes an infantry unit wearing jungle hats and camouflage, then a police constabulary platoon from Wilhelmsville. Troops from other colonies follow, the 1st Togo Pioneers, the Cameroonian Border Guard. Erica squeals in delight when she sees an elephant at the fore of the East African Pioneers. I must say these native troops seem as professional and disciplined as any German troops on parade. They could march with the 16th Bavarian RIR for certain.

Then come several African bush cars, the famous vehicles designed by Volkswagen for operating in the Serengeti. They are boxy and can seat up to six. One variant has treads, while another has massive wheels that keep the chassis more than a meter off the ground. Erica is fascinated by the light tanks and armored cars that come next. These are completely different from the heavy tanks used by Panzer divisions in the east, which would not be much use in the Congo jungle. Instead, these tanks are small and fast with a light gun. One tank is painted a desert gold and another jungle green.

Aggie kneels down next to Erica and points to the brochure in her hand, 'Hey Erica, you know what comes next?'

The wide-eyed girl, already overwhelmed by today's display, shakes her head.

'Airplanes!'

Erica jumps up and down and claps her hands in delight.

Indeed, one can feel the anticipation in the crowd. To announce the beginning of the aerial portion of the parade a Messerschmitt 303 fighter jet flies right over the Tiergarten, its roaring jet turbines drowning out all other sound. Erica cries and puts her hands over her ears. The crowd cheers and claps and shouts after the delta-winged fighter. The jet roars overhead and then banks sharply into the sky.

Another fighter jet soars past, this one from the Kriegsmarine. Then come the bombers, a quartet of four-engine Heinkel Mark Vs. They are massive, and their wingspan would easily cover the breadth of the Friedrichstrasse. These are the Luftwaffe's vaunted strategic bombers. They can fly deep into Russia and back, past Moscow even. Many in the Luftwaffe insist that their bombers have rendered obsolete the Wehrmacht's collection of armored and mechanized divisions and they can win a war with Russia simply by bombing Moscow to smithereens. Of course, no one has ever tried, so no one really knows.

Aggie says, 'Now you are in for a treat!' She points to a picture in the brochure of an older Messerschmitt, a 202 I think. It is painted orange and black and beneath the photo a caption exclaims, 'Valkyries!'

A minute later, the Luftwaffe's world famous aerial acrobatic squadron flies over the crowd. Four orange and black jets break in four different directions and re-form high in the sky. They take up a finger four formation and fly back over the crowd.

As the Valkyries impress the gawking public, in my mind's eye I see a series of paintings. These will commemorate this celebration next to the victory parade in which I marched in 1916. After all, today these men are marching across the exact same ground we marched in 1916. Already I can see a painting of the colonial contingents marching with dignity and pride down the Friedrichstrasse, a testament to the long term success of the German Empire and its civilizing mission. Perhaps the background is slightly darker than the rest of the scene, showing the struggle to get to this point, while the colonial contingents march toward a slightly brighter part of the canvas showing the future.

It is then that I notice a young black couple walking down the road past the throngs of people cheering on the parade. I recognize them, it is Josephine and Lionel from the Congo Pavilion. They are walking quickly and really have no business walking on the street. It is then I realize that something is very wrong. I see Lionel reach into his pocket. He holds something black in his hand. For a moment I fear it is a pistol. Lionel pulls an antenna out of the box and flips a switch. I actually see an orange light on the box.

I nudge Aggie, 'Get down!' I say.

'What?'

I nudge her again, 'Get down!'

'Why, Erica loves these jets, see, I...'

Most rudely I interrupt Aggie, 'Please, Aggie, a bomb is about to explode!'

'Whatever are you talking about?'

'Look,' I point to Lionel and Josephine. 'Those two, they have a bomb. Look at his hand.'

I am afraid that in my worry and haste I am unable to get my meaning across to Aggie.

'What's he talking about, Mommy?' Erica asked.

As Aggie tells her daughter not to worry and to enjoy the aerial show I hear distant gun fire. Most in the crowd are unaware of the gunfire, but when one has heard gunfire for real, one stays attuned to it. Then there is an explosion and another. Then the distant rip of a machinegun. By now, a few people are looking at one another wondering what the commotion is all about.

'Why start fireworks now?' a young woman asks her father.

The father actually looks worried and it is clear to me that he, too, has been under fire. I see smoke rising from the general area of the Kaiser's review stand. I look toward Lionel and Josephine, still walking briskly down the street. Just then Lionel presses a button. A moment later a large explosion rocks the crowd. People scream and shout. I see Lionel and Josephine running now down the street toward the reviewing stand. Then a stream of bullets slam into both of them, Lionel and Josephine fly backward onto the asphalt. In seconds the road beneath them runs red with their blood.

By then people all along the Tiergarten are panicking. Some try to run away from the street, while the smarter people duck. I see that Aggie has crouched down, her arms tight around Erica who is screaming. Behind them, the Congo Pavilion, or I should say the former Congo Pavilion, is in flames and spewing black smoke. Two black-suited German men kneel beside the bodies of Lionel and Josephine. One checks their pulses. The other, his sub-machinegun at the ready, scans the area for trouble. Then I hear a police siren and then another. Two police cars come thundering down the Tiergarten toward the Kaiser's review stand. People are now clearing out of the Tiergarten. I look about and see several victims lying on the ground being attended to by others. Past the armed men I see smoke and several men running about in front of the Kaiser's Pavilion.

'Do you think it's over?' Aggie asked.

'Mommy!' Erica cries.

I look around one last time. 'Ja.'

'We should go home.'

'One moment please.'

I hold out my hands and walk very slowly toward the two black-suited men kneeling beside Lionel and Josephine. The man with the submachine holds up his hand and shouts, 'Halt!'

I stop a few meters from him.

'What are you doing, mein Herr?' he asks. 'Please do not interfere.'

'I spoke with these two yesterday at the Congo Pavilion.'

'Is that true?'

I give the men my name and address. 'There I can be contacted, ja.'

'Ja,' the man nods. 'Thank you, mein Herr. Now please...'

'Of course.'

We hurry back home through streets emptying of people. Several police cars pass us and then most shockingly, army trucks filled with soldiers. When we get to the hallway, we hear the Bakers' phone ringing. It stops for a moment and then starts ringing again.

'That must be Bob,' Aggie says as she shakily fumbles in her purse for her keys. 'He must be worried sick.'

She rushes in and picks up the phone, 'Bob!' she says. 'Yes...yes...we just got back. No, we're ok...really, promise....no, he's fine. You have to go, Ok.'

She turns to me and says, 'That was Bob.'

'He wanted to know you and Erica were alright.'

'He's been worried sick.'

'Of course, he loves you both,' I say.

'He's going to be at the embassy all day, he says. Probably all night, too.'

'I would imagine,' I say. 'Now, are you and Erica, alright?'

Aggie looks at her daughter, who is already in her room playing with a doll. The child will be fine. Aggie nods.

'And you?'

'I'm a little shaken up.'

'Understandable....'

Just then I feel my knees buckle, I stagger and put a hand on the couch to prop myself up.

Aggie runs toward me and moves to the couch. I put a hand on my chest and breathe.

'Are you having a heart attack?' she asks.

I breathe deeply. 'Nein,' I say. My knees wobble. Then I laugh. 'I have not had a surge of adrenaline like that since....' I think back, 'Well at least since my time in Congo.'

'Oh.'

'That is the last time I was under fire.'

Aggie gets me a glass of water. I drink gratefully. As I sit on the couch regaining my composure, Aggie turns on the television. The news division has taken over the channel broadcast of course. The anchor talks while next to him a box shows live footage of the Tiergarten and reviewing stand. One half of the stand is a charred ruin. Before the stand, a polizei car and a Mercedes limousine burn out of control. Several bodies lie in various positions around and on the reviewing stand. I can see at least two black people dead on the street and one man in a dark gray suit, a member of the Kaiser's security detail, no doubt.

The screen switches to a live shot from the reviewing stand. Here is a reporter, his suit jacket is gone, as is his tie, his face smeared with soot. He stands awkwardly for several seconds as a helicopter passes overhead drowning out his own voice. After the helicopter passes the reporter says, 'We still do not know exactly what has happened. Only that several terrorists attacked the Grand Review. Behind me is the reviewing stand where both the Kaiser and the Chancellor were seated. I have been told by a police captain that both Kaiser Wilhelm and Chancellor Speer are unharmed.'

'Where are they now?' asked the news anchor.

'All the police captain would say is that both are in a, and I quote, safe place.'

Good, I think. I hope they are surrounded by a Prussian Guards battalion.

'Several bystanders have been killed. We do not at this time know how many. But viewers can see several bodies behind me.'

Indeed two figures limply lay on the rafters.

'Do we know anything about the victims?'

'Not at this time,' replies the reporter on scene.

'What about the perpetrators?'

'Ja. All we know is that they all seem to be black.'

'So Mobutu, then?'

'Possibly,' says the reporter on scene. 'But right now, that is just speculation.'

'Quite right,' says the anchor in studio. 'What other facts do we have?'

'Well, they attacked the Congo Pavilion as well. I'm afraid many people were killed or injured.'

I turn to Aggie, 'They're right, it has to be Mobutu.'

'I think that's jumping to conclusions,' she says.

'Nein, nein,' I reply. 'I talked to a pair of Congolese there the other day. They are now dead. The police shot them.'

'How horrible!' Aggie says, aghast. 'The police shot them simply because they are black!'

I can see Aggie is getting angry. Given the excitement and trauma she has just suffered, that is quite understandable. I do not press the point.

'I just hope they have killed or captured the perpetrators,' I say.

Even Aggie cannot disagree with that, and she nods. The studio anchor is thinking the same and asks, 'What of the people who carried out this attack? What has happened to them?'

'I do not know and the police captain with whom I spoke had no information. The polizei are very active. I do not know if you can hear, but sirens are blaring and a few minutes before we came on air my cameraman said he heard gunfire. So it would seem the police believe suspects are still at large.'

'Is there a threat to the wider public?' the studio anchor asks.

'Impossible to say. But what I can say is that the streets are filling up with machinegun-armed polizei and we have even seen troop transports.'

'Presumably from the Prussian Guards barracks.'

'Ja.'

I look over at Aggie, she is trembling. I put a comforting hand on her shoulder.

'This whole thing is awful,' she says. She continues trembling.

'Perhaps a drink?' I offer.

'Come now,' she sputters. 'It is not even noon.'

I look at Aggie very seriously. 'My dear. I have been in combat. I have experienced exactly what you are experiencing now. A small drink to steady your nerves, that is all.'

Aggie thinks for a moment.

'I think you're right.'

I wink, 'We shall not tell anyone.'

Finally, she laughs.

Aggie says there is gin in the liquor cabinet. I get a glass and fill it a quarter of the way with English gin, get a few ice cubes from the freezer and top it off with water. I hand Aggie the glass, she drinks.

'There,' I say, 'not too fast now.'

She laughs again. Aggie continues to tremble, so much so that the ice in the glass rattles. 'Here,' I offer, 'I shall hold the glass.'

Aggie takes another sip and begins to cry. 'It's just we were so close, and Erica…'

Now she sobs and falls back against the couch. 'I wish Bob was here.'

I pat her shoulder. 'Now your husband is an important official of the embassy and Ambassador Brundage needs him.'

Reluctantly she nods. 'I just feel…like those terrorist could barge in here and…'

'I know…' I say. 'I know…'

I realize that I can help. 'Would you excuse me, for one minute?' I ask. 'Will you be alright?'

Aggie nods.

I go to my apartment and ring up Peter Wulfe. He picks up and I tell him about what has happened. 'Ja, I see the news,' he replies.

'I wonder if you could help me. You recall Aggie?'

'That nice American woman, of course.'

'Well I was wondering…'

Twenty minutes later I am back at Aggie's apartment and hear a knock on the door. I answer. There stand Peter and Karl. Both have slender bags over their shoulders. I invite them in.

'Oh!' Aggie remarks. 'What are you two doing here?'

'Frau Baker,' Peter says. 'Our friend here says you are scared of the terrorists.'

'Well…I ….'

'It is alright,' Karl says. 'We are here to…keep you company.'

'Ja,' Peter adds. 'And if they come here and make trouble, we are prepared.' Peter unslings his bag and takes out a hunting rifle.

'Oh!' Aggie says.

'Forgive my brother his impudence. He and I both brought our hunting rifles. Just in case.'

I can tell Aggie is made uncomfortable by the rifles. So can Karl. He says, 'Frau Baker, we were both soldiers and hunters. We are weapons experts. I give you my word, you and your daughter are perfectly safe.'

Aggie nods. 'You are right.'

Erica comes out of her bedroom. 'Mommy! Look! Those nice men…and a gun!'

'Erica!'

'Can I see? Can I see?'

Peter says, 'If you approve, ma'am.' He opens up the breach. 'You see, it is unloaded.'

'Well…'

Erica has a grand time looking at Karl's rifle and loves working the bolt action. Aggie draws the line at Erica actually holding the rifle to fire, but grudgingly allows her to pull the trigger if the rifle is in Karl's lap. Otherwise Aggie, Peter and I watch the news, but over the course of several hours the reporters learn nothing at all.

'I do not understand why they aren't reporting anything new, just the same thing over and over again.'

Karl nods his head. 'Ja, this is smart.'

'Huh?' Aggie asks.

'They do not want to let the terrorists know what they know.'

'Ah!' I say.

'We used to do things like that all the time in Kindu.'

'Let me ask you something.'

'Of course, mein Herr.'

'Do you think Mobutu's men are capable of this?'

'Oh, absolutely!'

Aggie interrupts, 'We don't know it's Mobutu's men.'

'Frau Baker…' Karl begins, but one cross look from me persuades him not to argue with the fragile American woman. 'I saw them, well…I cleaned up the mess after Mobutu's men did things like this. They are most capable of this kind of terrorist attack. The question is, how were they able to execute such a complex operation over here?'

Karl says, 'They had help.'

Peter thinks for a moment and nods. 'Ja, they had help.'

And so we pass the afternoon watching the news and learning nothing. Aggie insists on cooking dinner for Karl and Peter. Being bachelors, the two men could use a home-cooked meal. Soon after, the phone rang. It was Bob telling Aggie he'd be home soon. She went about fixing something for her husband and this was good. Erica set the table for her mother.

When Bob comes home he looks tired but invigorated, there's a light in his eyes.

'Hey, Aggie,' he says almost dreamily. 'I spoke to the president.'

For the first time since the attack, Aggie looks happy. 'You spoke to the president?'

He nods, 'Yep, uh-huh! He asked Ambassador Brundage what German media was reporting and since I had been monitoring the television news, Brundage suggested he talk to me. The president said 'put him on.' Next thing I know I have the receiver and I'm telling President Kennedy about the German news.'

'What did he say?'

'Nothing much, just a lot of yeah and uh-huh and thanks, Baker. The ambassador was pleased too.'

I say, 'I think I had better go.'

'Ja, us too, says Karl.'

'But I haven't finished,' his brother says.

Karl grabs his brother by the arm. 'Let's go, chunk-head.'

'Thank you so much,' Aggie says.

I bow. 'Not at all. It was a most interesting day.'

Outside in the hallway I say to the brothers. 'That was a good deed you performed.'

'We got fed,' Peter says.

'Is that all you can think about?' asks Karl.

'I just meant she took care of us, is all.'

Karl thought for a moment. 'In your own idiotic way, you are right,' he says.

'Well you two should not think of it in that manner. You are good men doing a good thing.'

Karl shrugs. 'I suppose. But…'

'But what?' I ask.

'Nothing can ever make up for my deeds in the Congo.'

I pat Karl on the shoulder. 'You are a good man and a good soldier.'

'Thank you, mein Herr. Good evening.'

I return to my apartment, exhausted from a hectic day. Later, in bed, I ponder Peter's words about the terrorists, 'They had help....'

CHAPTER 4

———

'CHANCELLOR SPEER IS IN CONSTANT contact with local law enforcement,'
says the news reporter.

In studio the anchor replies, 'What has he been told?'

'The polizei have told the Chancellor that fourteen terrorists took part in
yesterday's attack. At least three are in custody.'

The Tiergarten is closed and ringed with troops. So I spend all day at
the Bakers watching television with Aggie. I have always recalled the dramatic events of 1914, but I experienced them through the paper and the town
square. Here, as events are unfolding on live television, it is most unique experience. We learn overnight that police have apprehended two of the terrorists
and killed several more in a bloody flop-house shootout.

International condemnation of the terrorist attack was swift. Here, the
local news anchor shows copies of the British papers which expressed shock,
outrage and disgust at the act. The Americans were in a tizzy. Even the
Russians expressed revulsion at the attempt on the Kaiser and Chancellor.
Moscow would never countenance such an act. Who would?

As we were watching the news report, the phone rings. It is Bob of course,
telling Aggie that he will not be able to come home that night. Given the crisis
at hand, Aggie says she understood.

'How is Bob?'

'Very busy,' Aggie says. 'He's monitoring German media and reporting to
Washington. Once this morning and once after lunch.'

'Since Bob will not be here,' I ask, 'would you like me to have Peter and
Karl over?'

Aggie blushes and smiles. 'Oh no, that was very sweet of you but I don't think that is necessary.'

I smile myself and nod. 'Quite right. The streets are full of police and troops.'

'Those troops bother me,' says Aggie.

'You have just not seen them before.'

'What are they afraid of?' Aggie asked.

'A repeat of 1914. That assassination led to a war.'

'But you won.'

I thought of what could have happened had we not won a quick victory over France and then turned around and smashed Russia. The thought of a long war with those kinds of weapons makes me sick.

I am thinking I will avoid Herr Weder's café, I just cannot stand the thought of him hectoring me about the obvious. But it would be rude, I think. I head down to his café for my morning coffee. *Der Spiegel* proclaims in 12 point letters: <u>Francs Found on Terrorists</u>.

'My god, are they that stupid?' I say aloud

Frau Weder comes out and pours my coffee. 'Where is Herr Weder?' I ask.

Frau Weder shakes her head. 'He is so angry he can barely leave the apartment.'

I laugh. 'I am sorry, Frau Weder,' I say. 'I do not mean to make light of your husband, or this terrible situation.'

'Please, I have done much worse than laugh at him. I wish he would find something else with which to fill his time.'

At this I say nothing.

That afternoon I am just lying down for my nap when I hear a furious knock at my door. It is Aggie.

'Did you hear?' she says most urgently, perhaps forgetting that I do not own a television.

'No I am afraid not,' I say.

'The polizei raided one of the terrorist's apartments and found a cache of weapons and explosives.'

'Oh dear!' I say, though this is obvious.

'They also found stacks of French francs.'

'Stacks?' I reply.

'Yes, thousands and thousands of francs!'

'I find that hard to believe.'

'Come see,' says Aggie. 'It is all over the news.'

Indeed, German media is breathlessly reporting that the Mobutu terrorists stashed thousands of francs at one of their safe houses. This strikes me as so incredibly dumb as to be implausible. Nevertheless, the news has footage of a polizei captain giving a tour of the safe house, making sure to show a cardboard box full of French francs. The next report reveals that forensics teams have found fragments of French-made explosive detonators.

'Where do you think they got francs and French-made explosives?' asks Aggie.

I reply that I do not know. Not wanting to worry Aggie, I do not say what I suspect. Nothing good can come of this information. Of this, I am sure.

The next morning *Der Spiegel* proclaims: <u>Russia Urges Restraint</u>.

This is nothing new. The previous day, *Der Spiegel* told us that 'Moscow Urges Caution', the day before, Moscow called for talks. After reading the lead story, I turn inside the paper and read an analysis of Moscow's intentions. So far, the columnist says, Moscow is being studiously neutral, and argues that this is a smart stance. Indeed, while Russia has vast armies, it also has vast and problematic expanses to police. Always, Moscow must worry about Mohammedan separatists in the Caucasus and a growing movement among the Mongoloids of Siberia for unification with their cousins in China. Even with the west in turmoil, Russia must tread lightly. The columnist is right, though. Much of what happens next will be determined by Moscow. Should Russia decide to back France, it would probably mean peace. After all, the General Staff cannot possibly want a two-front war, even with the Eastern Alliance of Poland, Hungary and Romania to support Germany. This is my hope. It seems strange to want Moscow to support Paris in this crisis, especially after having fought the Russians. But only a fool would want a new war.

In the Reichstag there are plenty of these.

All week I dread going to Weder's for my morning coffee and newspaper for fear of one headline. I see that headline in five inch block letters across *Der Spiegel's* front page -<u>MOBILIZATION!</u> Dread permeates my stomach. It is deep and heavy and bile rises in my throat. So much so that when Frau Weder comes to my table I wave her off.

'Oh, I cannot face this morning.'

Frau Weder nods her head. 'Neither can I.'

'No?'

'Our own Tomas was called up last night.'

'Oh,' I say.

'Johann is seeing him off today.'

Looking around, I do see a lack of young men. No doubt, those not being called up are rushing to the big recruiting office next to the General Staff Building. 'How is Herr Weder taking the news?'

'He is at once excited at the prospect of military action, but nervous for our son. As am I.'

'It will be alright, Frau Weder,' I say, hopefully in a reassuring manner.

'Do you think Tomas will be alright?'

'I know so,' I say. 'First, while the General Staff has begun mobilization, that may only be as a precaution and a bit of sabre rattling. Second, mobilization takes weeks and months.'

'Soooo....'

'So Tomas may simply be called to his depot and sit in barracks until the crisis subsides.'

'I hope so.'

By the evening *Der Spiegel* is running a new headline, 'CONSERVATIVE CALL FOR ACTION' reads the lead. 'Demand High Seas Fleet Sail.'

With the French fleet already at sea, it is risky for our own fleet to sally out of port. Unfortunately, Chancellor Speer agrees with the Reichstag warriors. The next day an entire squadron of four battleships sails out from Wilhelmshaven, comes around Dogger Bank in the North Sea and then heads back to port. The move is big news on the television and radio, and at the Bakers' I watch a long statement from the British Foreign Minister, Mr. Heath on the matter. Mr. Heath did not formally condemn the sortie by the Kriegsmarine, but he did convey that Her Majesty's government was very concerned about the escalation on the part of both nations. The statement is long and boring and Erica was bouncing off the walls the entire time Mr. Heath spoke.

We watch the news report without Bob and would do so for several days. He is busy at the embassy and was sleeping on a cot in Ambassador Brundage's office. Each day he makes time to call home at lunch and then again at dinner. In this way, I get something of an insider's account of what was happening from the American point of view. Nightly, Bob briefs the president on what German media was saying. Bob isn't able to tell Aggie very much, but it is clear that President Kennedy is deeply concerned about events here in Europe and is trying to take a central role in defusing the crisis. This is very unusual as the Americans have not taken an interest in European affairs since the Great War. Even without speaking to him directly, I can tell Bob takes tremendous professional pride in his new duties. So does Aggie, her eyes positively lite up every time she relates Bob's retelling of the nightly briefing.

As I feared, the situation is growing worse, seemingly by the hour. In response to the Kriegsmarine's Dogger Bank sortie, a Marine Nationale Flotilla of two battleships and several cruisers sallies out of their big naval base of Brest, sails through the English Channel and into the North Sea. Not surprisingly, in London, Whitehall expresses 'grave concern' at this move, urgent words indeed from the permanently temperamentally restrained foreign ministry. The next day our own Kriegsmarine once more sorties out into the North Sea, after which the Marine Nationale Flotilla sails again through the Channel to counter the Kriegsmarine. By this point Whitehall is perturbed and on advice of the Admiralty dispatches a task force from Scapa Flow to patrol the Channel. Since not even the most ardent navalists in the Kriegsmarine or Flotilla Nationale think they could take on the Royal Navy. Both Paris and Berlin decide to keep their fleets in port.

Which is not to say the military posturing stopped. Because the French army was on maneuvers during Victory Week, they have already amassed a force of a hundred thousand men in two army corps north of Paris. As a result, the General Staff believes the Wehrmacht is at a huge disadvantage and rushes troops to Alsace-Lorraine to make up the difference. In response, the French army holds a maneuver along the banks of the Loire in which French commanders show that the army can get one of its supposedly advanced armored divisions across the river in 12 hours. This implies that they could send an armored division across the Meuse River and into Alsace-Lorraine. Always waiting to be answered was the Russia question. So far Moscow's public utterings had been coy and noncommittal.

It was not until four days after the attack of the Grand Review, Bob is able to come home.

Aggie invites me over for dinner during which I inquire, 'Excuse me for asking, Bob, but why is your President Kennedy taking such an interest in this crisis?'

Bob wearily laughs. 'You promise not to tell anyone?'

'Ja,' I reply.

Bob smirks, 'No offense, but who would you tell?'

'Ja, a seventy-five year old artist. Who would I tell?' Herr Weder, I suppose.

'Sorry.'

'Quite all right.'

'Ok,' says Bob. 'You didn't hear it from me. But the president believes that if he can negotiate an end to the crisis…'

'Ahhhhh!' I say. 'Then that will help his reelection prospects.'

'His political people, Sorenson, White, they think a successful negotiation will assure victory.'

'I should think that is true.'

'Not only that, but it would put him in the running for a Nobel Peace Prize, like President Roosevelt won in 1906 for negotiating an end to the Russo-Japanese war.'

'One would be hard-pressed to argue against such an honor.'

'That's how he sees it,' Bob replies. 'And, to top everything off, if President Kennedy stops a war, it will mark the entry of the United States into European politics and even make us first among equals with Britain and Germany.'

Aggie, who up till then has been only eager to see her husband, says, 'I think that is horribly cynical.'

Bob shrugged.

'What about the Russians?' I ask.

'Ahhhh,' Bob says. 'Nobody knows what Moscow will do. I don't think Moscow knows what it will do.'

They are playing the waiting game.

The next morning I awake to news that the situation had worsened over-night. On the radio an announcer tells us, 'Early this morning jet aircraft of the Luftwaffe engaged several jet aircraft of the French air force. The Chancellor's office says French aircraft violated German territory while Paris vehemently denies the allegation. Exact numbers are unknown at this time, but the Chancellor's office confirms that both sides suffered losses.'

They are just bound and determined to have their war, I say to myself. Neither side agrees to a stand down, so for the next several days the frontier is bustling with military activity. Garrisons are beefed up, ammunition stocked and most importantly, several German divisions arrive in Alsace-Lorraine.

The French, of course, have responded in kind. Their two army corps move out from the maneuver area northeast of Paris and east toward the fron-tier, finally settling in the across the border from Sedan. From here, the two French army corps can move into Belgium should the General Staff choose to repeat the Schlieffen Plan of 1914, or south against the Wehrmacht right flag, should they cross the frontier south of Belgium.

With a quarter million French troops on one side of the border and a quarter million German troops on the other side of the border, the negotia-tions, which thus far had been behind closed doors, became very public. In this case, it is the English speaking peoples who work feverishly to avoid war. President Kennedy negotiates personally with President de Gaulle. For the Americans to work with Paris only makes sense. Since 1914 the French have deeply mistrusted the British, feeling that Whitehall abandoned them in the face of the advancing German army. Ever since, France has maintained a cold distance to Britain. For their part, the British have always been indifferent to France, their military alliance having brought London nothing but trouble. The Americans have always maintained warm relations with the French.

While President Kennedy works with de Gaulle, Prime Minister MacMillon is in constant contact with Chancellor Speer.

That night I watch the news with Aggie.

After a day of furious negotiations, the English Foreign minister holds a press conference at Whitehall in which he announced, 'I have spent most of the day in contact with Chancellor Speer. I have just now gotten off the telephone with him. The conversations were exhaustive and focused solely on putting an end to the current European crisis. Throughout, Chancellor Speer relayed his concerns and also listened to what Her Majesty's government had to say. I have here in my hand a list of points Chancellor Speer hammered out with me. He will have an exact copy in Berlin. Here they are.

'First, as to the current crisis, the German government agrees to withdraw all troops from the frontier so long as the French government does the same. The Chancellor has told me that he will make the first move if this will help start the process. Chancellor Speer calls for the grounding of all aircraft in the Rhine and Meuse River Valleys to avoid a repeat of the tragedy there a few days prior. He also will keep the German fleet in port if the French fleet does the same. Chancellor Speer expects France to make the first move on this point as a gesture of good will.

'Secondly as to the attack on the Grand Review, Germany calls for an international commission to investigate the attack. The commission will be chaired by Great Britain and the United States....

'What does that mean,' Aggie asks. She sees me smiling. 'Why are you so happy?'

'Because it would seem the war hawks in the Speer Ministry are losing.'

'How can you tell?'

'Easy, my dear,' I say. 'This international commission. It seems too reasonable. You Americans, always so eager to help, will no doubt eagerly help here. And the British, well, they will be thorough, professional, and honest.'

'Why would the hawks oppose that?'

'Oh, I don't think they would, necessarily. If they really wanted a war, they would insist on an investigation run by our own polizei.'

'Ohhhh...' Aggie says. 'Paris would never accept that.'

I smile to myself, admiring the way this American housefrau is able to put two and two together and understand the situation before her.

'Exactly, my dear,' I say. 'In 1914, the Austrian government made just that demand of the Serbians. Belgrade said no, of course, and the result was war.'

Having spent the last week dreading the prospect of war with France, after the news I go to bed feeling good. The good feeling dissipates with the morning radio report which states that Paris has categorically rejected the

Speer government's call for an international investigation. At Weder's Café I see the headline writers at *Der Spiegel* are having fun. The front of the paper declared, 'de Gaulle to Speer: Merde.'

After the news, I was in no mood to paint and instead went to the Bakers'. Television seems the best way to follow events. Aggie is watching television, which is given over to twenty four hour coverage of the unfolding crisis. Here we saw a news anchor with a civilian military analyst.

'Last night Paris announced the call up of 30-day reservists…What exactly does that mean?' asked the in-studio news anchor.

Replies the analyst, 'It means the French are mobilizing their secondary divisions. Most likely their primary divisions are filled out and ready for action, probably with standing troops from those secondary divisions. With this 30-day call up, the French army hopes to fill in the gaps left by the cannibalization of the secondary divisions.'

'Does this mean they are preparing for war?'

'Most certainly.'

Says Aggie, 'Oh, my god! Can they really want that?'

I think about Speer's perfectly reasonable offer. What more could Paris want? Unless they want war, but that seems unthinkable. We have more people and a larger army. At least in 1914, France went to war knowing England was at her back. But here she stands alone.

'Aggie,' I say. 'I honestly do not know what the French want. It makes no sense to me.'

On the floor by Aggie's chair, Erica draws pictures and colors them in with crayons. When she finishes she hands it to me. It is a picture of several soldiers, clad in gray, and marching. 'Just like you!' she exclaims.

'Thank you, *liebchen*,' I pat Erica's head. 'But that was a long time ago. In fact…'

'Shhh!' Aggie says. She points to the television where the screen has switched from the news studio in Berlin to the presidential podium in Washington, DC. Aggie looks on in such great interest, it seemed almost sexual.

After pleasantries the president says, 'This morning, after the announcement of the French rejection of Chancellor Speer's proposal, I am offering to personally conduct one-to-one negotiations between President de Gaulle and Chancellor Speer, here in Washington or at another place agreeable to both parties. After consultations with London, Prime Minister MacMillon has suggested Geneva as a possible meeting place. I will fly there immediately if requested to do so.

'As Europe lurches toward war, as President of the United States I urge both Germany and France to step away from the brink before it is too late. Almost exactly fifty years ago, Europe was at a similar point and the failure of all sides to come to a reasonable accommodation led to two years of war...'

I shake my head.

'You see, here is the President's problem,' I say, 'to us Germans, he is invoking a successful and glorious military conflict. To the French, he is reminding them of their need for a war of revenge.'

'Well, at least he is trying to foster peace!' Aggie snaps. Whether she is upset that the president's peace efforts are failing or that I am interrupting his speech, I cannot say.

'Oh, I agree with you, Aggie,' I say. 'Remember, I was a soldier in the last war.'

'Oh, you're right,' Aggie says. 'I'm so sorry.'

'Not at all.'

Not long after, Bob comes home. His tie is undone, shirt sleeves rolled up and blazer slung over his shoulder. Deep bags are beneath his eyes. He looks positively exhausted.

'The chief of staff ordered us all to go home,' he says.

'Why?' Aggie asks. 'During a time like this.'

'He said we all need to be rested and ready.'

I nod. 'Wise.'

'Like I said, he ordered me home.'

Aggie fixes Bob a small meal while Erica crawls into his lap. She missed her father. Bob eats and told us about what was happening.

'I am not privy to everything,' he says as he puts a forkful of vegetables in his mouth, 'But Ambassador Brundage spends half the day on the phone with President Kennedy and the other half on the phone with Chancellor Speer.'

'What does Chancellor Speer say?' Aggie asks.

Bob bounces Erica on his knee as he speaks. 'Right now, the Chancellor is under enormous pressure from the General Staff to act. They are terrified of a two-front war.'

I nod my head. 'Ja. It was the same in 1914.'

'Their nightmare is going to war with France and Russia at the same time.'

'War!' Aggie exclaimed. 'Is it really that serious?'

'I'm afraid it is.'

'You were there in 1914?' Bob asks. 'Is this what it was like?'

'Ja. We had war fever. And we had to defeat France as quickly as possible so we could turn around and defeat Russia. They were the real threat.'

Aggie says, 'But the Russians haven't done anything.'

'Not so far, no. But the General Staff must act as if they might.'

True, Russia has so far done nothing more than express their sympathies to the bereaved and satisfaction that the perpetrators have been caught. What they would do next is anybody's guess.

'Would you like some coffee?' Aggie asks her tired husband.

'Na, it will just keep me up.' Bob rubs his tired face again and sighs. 'I just don't get it,' he says. 'We know that French intelligence officials helped these Mobutu terrorists. The French have a responsibility to clean up this mess, everyone agrees. Washington, London, hell, I bet even Moscow!'

'Ja,' I say. 'This is probably why Moscow has been so silent.'

'Right,' Bob replies. 'There is no defending what the French have done here. Speer does not want a war. I know this, I have listened in on the conversations between Speer and Brundage. But the French have got to give him something.'

'It would be wise.'

'But they won't give an inch,' Bob says. 'It's almost as if they want a war...'

The morning news broke that in London, Whitehall announced a quarantine of the English Channel. Fearing some kind of incident at sea, the Royal Navy will cordon off the channel from Dover to Calais and forbid all naval traffic through it. Paris is outraged, of course, but Chancellor Speer sensibly announces that the Kriegsmarine will abide by the quarantine. This is only smart, no good could come of sending German warships through the channel, though no doubt some ambitious fools in the Kriegsmarine want to do just that.

There follows news from Paris that President de Gaulle will be making an emergency speech at noon. Aggie invites me over to watch.

As we wait for de Gaulle's speech, Aggie says, 'This must be it. An announcement from de Gaulle that he is accepting offers at mediation, something.'

In my opinion this is hope rather than conviction. I could not blame Aggie for that. She seems genuinely scared at the possibility of war - so much more sensible than the hawks in the Reichstag.

De Gaulle goes on air at about ten after noon. He is defiant, insisting that France had nothing to do with the terrorist attack and any evidence saying they did was manufactured by German authorities. He went on to declare that the French military mobilization would continue and France would defend her sacred soil to the end against any and all German encroachments.

'What is he saying?' Aggie asked.

I shake my head. 'I do not understand. It would be so easy for him to defuse this crisis. Is French pride so wounded after 1873 and 1914 that they will risk a war in 1964? It seems so.'

'Surely Chancellor Speer will not respond in kind?' Aggie says. 'Surely he will look to the international community for help.'

I reply, 'Chancellor Speer is a wise and level-headed leader.' I shake my head again. 'But every man, every nation has its breaking point. Germany's is her national honor and the French are besmirching it.'

'So you will kill thousands of young men for your national honor?' she mocks.

'I did not say I would do so, Aggie,' I reply. 'No one who has been shot at could be so eager. Please remember that.'

'You're right.'

'But there are too many in the Reichstag who have not been shot at and I fear they will prevail.'

Indeed, after de Gaulle's speech pandemonium reigns in the Reichstag. Some are calling for outright invasion. Others demanded Germany mount an effort against some of France's colonial possessions. Honestly, what do we want with Chad? At this point the more sensible and reasonable option seemed to be some sort of blockade. But again, to what end? Do we really want to take possession of French West Africa? Besides the French Marine Nationale would challenge such a blockade and I seriously doubt the Royal Navy would stand for such a disruption of the mid-Atlantic.

By the next morning, war is inevitable. I knew it because of the joint announcement by the Russian foreign minister and our own foreign minister, proclaiming that neither Germany nor Russia would mobilize their armed forces on their mutual frontier. This freed the General Staff from having to worry over and plan for war with Russia. Also it allows the General Staff to shift resources from east to west; petrol, rolling stock and the like. Indeed that night Bob comes home and tells Aggie that the embassy is offering trips back to America for the families of embassy personnel. Aggie refused. Though she is upset and worried, and seemingly personally devastated by the worsening news, she insists upon staying. This is smart actually and sensible as any good house frau would be. What chance existed of the war coming to Berlin?

CHAPTER 5

––––

AND SO WAR COMES, TWO days later.

Operationally the French are at a tremendous disadvantage. Our own Army of the Rhine operates out of the Rhine and Saar River Valleys. More importantly the fortress city of Metz is mere miles from the French border. This is the logistical hub for the I Army Corps of five divisions. These cross the border on 1 September and advance generally west, southwest on the line of Nancy to Troyes fifty miles to the west on the River Loire. At the same time II Army Corps of six divisions crosses the border and advances west-northwest toward Rheims. This advance puts II Corps in excellent position to secure the frontier against the two French Army corps known to lie on the Belgian border. This French deployment makes sense. They were in excellent position to enter Belgium, should the Wehrmacht decide to attack through Belgium, or swing south and engage advancing German forces head-on. Indeed for the first three days of the war, the northern wing of the German advance sees the majority of the fighting.

I sit at Otto's at night, watching the now 24 hour a day news reports. Correspondents ride into battle with German forces and send back photographs and film of the actual combat - remarkable. From what I see, war has not changed one bit in 50 years. Of course the tools are different. In 1914 we had no tanks and only a few aeroplanes. Now the skies are filled with aeroplanes shooting at one another or shooting at troops on the ground. All this mechanized equipment makes for a horrible mess. Each meeting of French and German forces leaves behind flaming junkyards of cars, trucks and Panzers. I suppose this is an improvement over the battlefields full of dying, braying horses that I walked across.

The battlefields of 1964 are moving in one direction, west. French forces are simply falling back, or being pushed back at a rate of five to ten kilometers a day till by the end of the first week of the war, lead elements of II Army Corps are on Rheims' outskirts and preparing to invade the city. This seems like a wise move on the part of the French. Though it must have been heart wrenching for them to abandon French soil, this move takes our forces away from their logistical base along the Rhine and Metz and brings the battle closer to French logistical bases around Paris.

Little is happening at sea. When the war began Whitehall announced that the Channel blockade is still in effect. While this no doubt annoyed the Kriegsmarine it is hard to blame the British for the declaration. They do not want a naval battle off their shores. In the south, the mighty Italian navy, certainly the best in the Mediterranean, closed off the central Mediterranean. So the Kriegsmarine sent several cruisers through the North Sea and into the Atlantic. In the Caribbean, a German U-boat sunk a French destroyer off Martinique, an action which greatly angered Washington, while a French cruiser sunk a pair of German destroyers in the Baltic, which Moscow protested. Aside from a few other small naval actions in the North Atlantic, so far the war at sea has been anti-climactic.

At the end of seven days, German forces have advanced more than sixty kilometers inside France. The map looks as if the Wehrmacht has advanced a thumb northwest into France and occupied a space between the Belgian border and the River Marne. Already Washington and London are calling for a ceasefire. I must say they have a point. The Wehrmacht has battered French forces and pushed them off the frontier. Several hundred square kilometers of French territory now under German occupation are leverage for Speer to negotiate. Why not talk?

On the eighth day of the war, bereavement notices start coming home. Unlike the Great War, the Wehrmacht is able to send the bodies of dead soldiers home to their loved ones. Dozens of notices arrive and dozens of funerals are held in Berlin alone. Streets that a week earlier were filled with joyous Berliners are giving way to funeral processions led by grieving mothers and widows draped in black. Sometimes a father or grandfather leads the casket, himself wearing an old uniform, or perhaps just a medal pinned to a black suit. Funerals like these take place throughout the country, and on the ninth day of the war, I watch at Otto's as the newscast led with a compilation of funerals, one in Berlin, one in Nuremburg, another in Munich. Clearly the entire nation is in mourning.

Nightly, France and Germany spar on television. Both sides are using the medium to communicate with one another. President de Gaulle gives a speech from the palace followed by a quick address from Chancellor Speer at the Chancellery. Reading between the lines has become something of a sport with the clientele at Otto's. As I am by far the oldest patron, the young people at Otto's presume I intuitively understand what is happening. I laugh to myself about this idea of an old artist being able to discern what is happening at the Chancellery and the Palace, but I tell the youths what I know. At times I become quite animated.

One young man named Gunther asks me questions about the French in the Great War and I tell him of my encounters with French POW's. Given the current situation, I answer the young man's questions as best I can and I finally tell him, 'Look, young fellow. I was only briefly on the Western Front and by the time we arrived the war was as good as won. I did not see any fighting until we went east.'

So he pesters me with questions about the Russians. What were they like? Could they fight? What was Russia like? And most importantly, did I think they would enter the war?

One night at closing Otto tells me, 'You know you are prone to going on for some time.'

'Really?'

'You just spent forty five minutes lecturing that youth on the French during the Great War.'

I look away, a bit embarrassed at my long-windedness. 'My apologies.'

'Do not apologize, my friend. Those young people hung on your every word. You kept them here, buying and drinking beer. I almost feel as if I should give you a percentage.'

I laugh.

When I get home Aggie invites me over. 'There has been some big news at the front!' she says.

I raise an eyebrow, 'Oh?'

'Yes,' she replies. 'And whatever is happening is really huge, Bob just called and said he won't be home tonight.'

'Hmmm…' I pondered. 'Something important is happening.'

We sit and watch the television. A reporter with the I Army Corps in France says the advance has come to a dead stop before Rheims.

'What prompted this?' asks the news anchor from Berlin.

'As you can see in the background, the French deployed some of kind of weapon,' the reporter on the ground points behind him.

From a distance the television screen shows a picturesque French coun-tryside, a dirt road, some hedgerows and a line of Panzers parked along the side. German soldiers stand around the tanks, talking, eating or smoking. The image would make a wonderful still life. But in the distance, difficult to say because the television gives one a warped perspective, a great cloud in the shape of a tree or mushroom pierces the sky.

'What is that?' Aggie asks.

'How many explosives did they use?'

'I do not know,' I shake my head. 'They would need a tremendous amount of TNT for something that big.'

The news anchor in Berlin asks, 'Can you describe what happened?'

'Yes, I was napping inside an armored personal carrier when a blast woke me up. I went outside and a concussion knocked me flat. The blast was so strong it rocked our APC back on its sprockets. Men were screaming about a blinding light that suddenly flashed and disappeared, I saw dozens of men screaming, holding their hands to their eyes. Suddenly they were blinded.'

'I do not know, I…'

'One moment, please,' says the news anchor. He pressed his earpiece and says, 'Our producer is telling me that President de Gaulle is about to speak. We will be going to him live, right now.'

The screen switches to the French Presidential Palace. De Gaulle stands at a podium, a row of French flags behind him. He looks solemn yet determined.

'Today the nation of France took rightful measures to defend the soil and the people of this great nation. Today we made use of the ultimate weapon…'

'Ultimate weapon?' Aggie asked.

'Today, in defense of our nation, our soil, our people, France deployed the *bombe atomique*…'

CHAPTER

———

Bob had not been home in two days. Aggie and I watched as the news anchor interviewed Professor Heisenberg about France's new bomb.

'The principle is simple,' says the professor. 'One uses uranium to split an atom which releases a tremendous amount of energy.'

'I see. But how can something so small contain such a massive amount of explosive power?'

'Well uranium is highly radioactive and splitting a uranium atom creates a chain reaction whereby more and more energy is released. We always knew this was possible, in theory. But now we know this theory is fact.'

The news anchor says, 'Let us show the footage released by the French government.'

The television shows grainy technicolor footage of a French tropical Pacific island. One sees sand, palm trees and crystal blue water. It looks like paradise. Then there is a flash of light and suddenly a horrific-looking orange and yellow fireball rising into the sky.

Heisenberg says, 'What you are seeing now is the result, an atomic fireball followed by a mushroom cloud billowing into the sky.'

'Just how powerful is this atomic blast?'

'The French claim the blast is equal to twenty tons of TNT.'

'What does that mean in layman's terms, professor?'

Heisenberg looked at some notes. 'According to the French, this produces a fireball with a radius of 260 meters and air blast zone of just over a kilometer, meaning anything within that perimeter will be flattened like a pancake.'

'We see reports of German soldiers with severe burns.'

'Ja, this would be a result of the radiation.'

'And blindness.'

'Ja, from the detonation. Remember, this caused a burst of light brighter than the sun.'

Beside me Aggie says, 'This sounds like a horrible weapon.'

All I could do was nod. 'It is.'

On the television the anchor asks, 'Professor, how many casualties have our forces suffered?'

'From this one blast?'

'Thousands initially and thousands more from the effects of radiation.'

'Really?'

'Yes. Recall that the Curies were poisoned by their own work on x-rays. The same principle is at work here. Thousands of German soldiers have been exposed to massive doses of radiation.'

'Meaning?'

'Meaning they will die.'

Aggie put her hands to her face, 'Oh my god,' she says.

'Professor Heisenberg,' began the news anchor. 'Does Germany have a comparable weapon?'

'Not that I know of.'

We later learn that two whole regiments of the Prussian Guards division were all but destroyed by this atomic bomb. The French targeting was quite clever. The Prussian Guards were leading the advance on Rheims. This was the best division in the Wehrmacht and its virtual destruction constituted a severe blow to national morale.

The day after his speech, President de Gaulle gives Chancellor Speer an ultimatum. Withdraw all troops from French territory within 72 hours or face further atomic attacks. The use of this new atomic weapon paralyzed the General Staff. They split into two factions, one that wants to halt the advance and consolidate, the other arguing that because of this new super weapon, the Wehrmacht should seek a decisive battle in France to win the war. The result was dithering indecisiveness. The fighting continued though more timidly and mostly on I Corps' front. Here follow-on divisions pushed northwest around Rheims to isolate it from Paris.

The next day the 6th Bavarian Division is all but annihilated in an atomic attack.

I learn about this while enjoying a slice of cake at Otto's. Gunther and his friends just stare in amazement at the television images, a flash of light, a fireball and a mushroom cloud showing where the 6th Bavarian Division had been. Seeing the destruction and thinking of the carnage I wept openly at the destruction of my own division. Gunther put an arm around me and says, 'It will be alright, mein Herr.'

I look up at the billowing mushroom cloud on the television. 'I wish I could believe that.'

This talk of war and this new super weapon tire me. I pay my bill and go outside. Gunther follows.

A man standing outside Otto's is waving a German flag and shouting. 'On to Paris! On to Paris!' Before him gather a few dozen people shouting and chanting along.

'Ja, easy for him to shout when he is safe in Berlin.'

Gunther shouts, 'You go! You go! You go to Paris.' Beside him a few of his friends took up the chant. 'You go! You go! You go to Paris.'

The man with the flag sees Gunther and points at him.

'Look at that young man!' he shouts. 'He should be at the front!'

For a moment Gunther blushes. I wonder, who is this blowhard, calling for war from Berlin. This annoys me.

I shout back with ferocity. This surprised me. 'Why are you here?'

The man with the flag shouts back. 'I am here to support our troops in the field!'

'From Berlin?' I laugh.

'What do you know about it old man?'

I laugh again. 'I carried a rifle in 1914 and 1915, that is what I know!'

People turn from the man with the flag and look at me.

'Then you should know the importance of marching to Paris!'

'Should I?' I replied. 'I have been in battle. I have been shot at. I have shot men. Men I stood next to fell, their innards torn to shreds by a bullet or a piece of shrapnel.'

'I thank you!' the man with the flag shouts.

'And I have marched! Oh, have I marched! Across battlefields full of shattered young men, through towns reduced to rubble, past civilians who lost absolutely everything to the war we made and fought.'

People stop and watch.

'I do not understand what is happening,' I say. 'But I do know this "on to Paris" jingoism is going to get many young men killed. I do not want to see that.' In the crowd I see people nodding their heads and murmuring to each other. I must say the feeling is good. 'I do not want to see more young men die!' I repeat. 'Do you? Any of you?!'

People shake their heads.

I look at them, 'That is all I have to say. You follow this man if you like. I am going home.'

A few people clap. One man whistles.

The next night at Otto's we watch television. The news is bleak. Though the French have not detonated anymore of these super weapons, our forces have halted. The Reichstag is in chaos with a fist fight breaking out between a member of the Conservatives and the SPD. The General Staff seems paralyzed.

Otto stands on his side of the bar watching with me. He cleans a beer glass looks at me and says. 'Ja, this is not good.'

I shake my head. 'Nein.'

'Speer needs to get hold of this situation before we have a real crisis on our hands.'

'We already have a real crisis on our hands.'

Gunther walks in. Behind him are several young people, his friends I presume. Gunther points to me and says, 'That's him.'

A pretty young girl comes up to me and says, 'Excuse, mein Herr, I am sorry to bother you.'

'Not at all. How can I help you, my dear?'

'My name is Ingrid. I was watching you speak yesterday and I just wanted to say that I very much agree with what you said.'

'Well thank you, my dear.'

Behind the young fraulein, several other young people nod their heads.

She says, 'I was wondering if you could come speak to my youth group.'

'Me?' I reply. 'What on earth for?'

'Because I believe you made much sense, mein Herr, and I would like my friends to hear what you say.'

'I am just an old artist, an old man.'

'True, mein Herr. But you are better known on the streets of Berlin than you think. People see your work, they even purchase your work.'

'She is right, mein Herr,' Gunther says.

'I do not see what good I could do. Or why I would even be wanted.'

'Just to hear what a veteran of the last war has to say about this current crisis, mein Herr.'

'Ja,' says Gunther. 'It would mean a lot. We are surrounded by war enthusiasts. We hear war slogans. I myself was prepared to enlist until I heard you.'

'Are you saying that you no longer want to serve the Reich?' I ask.

'Nein, mein Herr. Simply that you made me think.'

'Ja, and now we would like you to make our friends think.'

I am going to politely decline, but these young people are asking for my help and I recall what the likes of Hermann Struck did for me and I nod my agreement.

Gunther and his friends take me to their music hall several blocks away. I know we are approaching the music hall because I hear live music, drums, bass, guitar and a voice imitating the latest English hits. We walk in. A large lad holding a ream of pamphlets hands one to me. *War!* It proclaims. *Will you do your part for the honor of Germany?! Find your local recruiter today!* Another young man hands me a pamphlet detailing the crimes of de Gaulle and France.

The hall seats a few hundred and it is filled to capacity. In fact, several dozen are standing in the back. The energy of youth reverberates throughout. Many of the young people are reading the pamphlets and discussing them among themselves. Young people talking, young men and women dancing most scandalously, here and there a young couple lean against a wall and kiss. Others simply enjoy the music. Several Reich flags are scattered throughout. I see the band on stage. They look like those young Englishmen currently ruining music and I am grateful when Gunther waves to the band and points to me. I see the lead singer nod. They finish the song and he waves his hand.

The lead singer says, 'Hey, cats. We all know what the big issue of the day is. Gunther, our manager has tracked down an old fellow who has something to say about the war. Some of you have seen him about. He's that old painter in the Tiergarten.'

The singer finishes his introduction. I walk down the aisle toward the stage. I hear the young people murmuring among themselves.

'I know that man!'

'What is he doing here?'

'Do we really need to hear this?'

'I came here for music.'

I take the stage. The young singer offers me the microphone but I did not want to hold that thing. The young people gradually stop talking and look up at me. I look back at them - young, eager faces smooth and lacking the ravages of age. Their eyes are wide as if I am about to give them distilled truth. For a moment I wonder if I ever looked this way. I must have. I look about one more time. The crowd before me has fallen utterly silent.

'One of your number asked me to come here to speak about the war and this crisis,' I begin. I fold my arms and look down at my feet for a moment to collect my words. 'I know what you are going through now. I was once a youth like you, fifty years ago as another great crisis befell Europe and I was called upon to serve my nation, just as you are now...'

I do not know how long I speak, ten minutes perhaps a little more. But by the time I finish, the young people stand and clap ferociously. I walk off stage and back through the door. Young people clap and smile, several pat me vigorously on my 75 year old back, nearly knocking me over. A young lady steps forward and takes my arm to steady me and helps me through the aisle to the entrance where Gunther and his friends wait.

Gunther says, 'Mein Herr, you captivated them!'

'Did I?'

'They hung on your every word.'

Ingrid, 'You should come back tomorrow.'

'I already said my piece,' I reply.

'And you should say it again, mein Herr.'

She turns from me to the young people now exiting the music hall. 'Tell all your friends!' she shouts. 'Tell everyone to come here tomorrow!'

'What time?' one person asks.

'Uhh…seven PM. Seven PM!' Ingrid shouts at the young people departing the music hall. 'Tell all to come at seven PM to hear this great man speak!'

She looks at Gunther and says, 'I have to go. I have so much to do.'

When I get home, Aggie comes over right away. She hasn't seen Bob all day and says he won't be coming home that night at all. Graciously she invites me for dinner. She is lonely.

Over dinner Aggie tells me what she's heard from Bob.

'He can't tell me much. He did say the president is extremely worried about this new bomb the French have.'

'As well he should be. This weapon is terrible.'

'Bob says half the talk from the White House is about how to stop the war, the other half is about how to make this new bomb. I think that is just awful.'

Pushing my food around my plate I say. 'It would be wise, no?'

'Wise?' Aggie asked incredulously. 'To have such a powerful bomb that goes on killing people even after it explodes? What a horrible thing!'

I nod and say, 'Yes, but if France were the only nation to have this bomb wouldn't they use it at their discretion?'

'Why…I….'

'And if they knew other nations had a similar weapon, would that not dissuade them from using it?'

Aggie looks down and purses her lips in thought.

'Ah,' I say, popping one of her stuffed mushrooms in my mouth. 'See. If everyone can use this wonder weapon…'

'Horror weapon!'

'Very well….Horror weapon. If everyone can use this horror weapon, as you call it, then no one will.'

'But it would be better if they did not exist.'

'Yes,' I reply. 'But they are a fact.'

The next morning I see a placard pasted to a lamp post announcing my speaking at the music hall. At the next street corner another lamp post has a bill announcing my speaking, as does the one after that and the one after that. As I look around I see bills on every lamp post, and every street corner. Then I notice a steady trickle of young people heading for the music hall. When I arrive at the hall I am shocked to see hundreds and hundreds of people are gathered. The entire sidewalk is packed with people and not just young people. I see the old, the middle-aged. I see many women with their children, no doubt their husbands are at the front. Sadly, perhaps a few of their husbands have been killed by now. Maybe even incinerated by this new bomb.

Gunther and Ingrid see me approaching. 'I am afraid we have a lot of spillover,' he points to all the people waiting outside the music hall.

'I see.'

Ingrid says, 'So I had a podium microphone set up out front.'

In front of the music hall entrance they have built an impromptu stage of cinderblocks and wooden planks. Gunther and Ingrid each take my arm and help me to the top of the podium. Gradually word spreads that I have arrived and people congregate in front of me. Soon the entire street is filled, as is the intersection. I have not been part of an assemblage of people like this since the war. It is larger than the entire 16th Bavarian Reserve Infantry Regiment for certain.

Ingrid steps up to the podium, tests the microphone and then introduces me. 'Many of you have seen this great man around Berlin. He is a painter, an artist, a man who has travelled widely in the world. He is also a veteran of the Great War. And he has important things to say about this war.' Impatiently, I wait for her to finish. This is not really necessary. When she finishes I take the podium to a cheering crowd. Then Ingrid starts chanting something - I cannot tell what, but Gunther joins her. Slowly the crowd takes up the chant and I can make it out, 'Peace now! Peace now!'

As the crowd chants on, I take time to collect my thoughts. The girl raises her hands and tamps the crowd down, gradually bringing them to silence. For several more seconds I say nothing. Finally I look up at the crowd. 'Fifty years ago...' I begin, 'I was standing in a square much like this one, amidst war fever and an international crisis...'

The crowd silently watches as I tell my tale. Halfway through my little talk, why be so modest - it is a speech - before...a few thousand it would seem,

I realize that a girl is filming me with a very expensive 8mm camera. I glance down at her and she nods. I continue.

As I near the end of my talk I realize that the crowd now extends past the intersection and well down the street. Hundreds more have joined to hear my talk. I also see at the intersection several polizei cars. Though the sirens do not wail, the lights turn about, announcing their presence. I see a half dozen polizei making their way through the crowd toward me. The crowd is made of young people, but they are still Germans and they respectfully make way for the authorities. A polizei officer comes to the podium and asks, 'What is this, mein Herr?'

Before I can answer him Ingrid explains, 'This is a peace rally.'

'Ja, fraulein,' the polizei officer says. 'Mein Herr?'

I reply, 'This is a peace rally.'

'This crowd must disperse at once!'

'How dare you!' Ingrid shouts.

'If the crowd does not disperse we will have to call for reinforcements.'

People around us start booing. There is a young mother with a baby stroller and she shouts, 'Why don't you arrest the people who began this war?'

Then Ingrid takes up the cause, 'Yes, that is a good question!'

The polizei, sensing the tense situation says, 'mein Herr?'

'Of course.' I do not want to see trouble. I speak into the microphone. 'Fellow Germans. We have said our piece. We have made our point. Let us now go home in peace.'

Ingrid boos but I remind her, 'These polizei are here to help us disperse in an orderly way. And we shall do so,' Thinking of the long history of French riots, I add, 'We do not live in Paris! We live in Berlin!' the crowd cheers. 'And we will act like good Germans, not disorderly French anarchists!' I raise my hands in the air and slam them down on the podium.

Gunther starts singing Deutschland Über Alles. In moments most of the crowd takes up our national anthem.

As the polizei officer and I walk through the singing crowd he says to me, 'Danke, mein Herr.'

'Not at all, officer,' I reply. 'I no more wish to see trouble than you do.'

'Danke.' He says. 'You know, I think you made many good points.'

The next morning my phone rings. It is Otto calling. 'Did you see it? Did you see it?'

'See what?' I ask.

'You were on television!'

'I was on television? How is that possible?'

'Your little speech at that peace rally. Someone brought a camera and gave the footage to the local news station!'

It was Ingrid, I realize.

'What did they show me doing?'

'The news excerpted part of your speech, the part where you talk about fighting in the Great War and not wanting to see more young men killed.'

'Really?' I say.

'Come down now. They will rerun the broadcast when this one is over, you know.'

Intrigued, I head down to Otto's in time for the bottom hour broadcast.

'Yesterday here in Berlin, a large demonstration occurred at a local music hall. A crowd of mostly young people gathered urging peace in the face of the European crisis. They also listened to one elderly man who was present during the last war, a local artist known in the German art world for his neo-classical work...'

There I am, standing at the podium speaking eloquently and fiercely, arms raised one moment, fists slamming down to the podium the next. I must admit that I enjoy seeing myself this way.

'It was those young people that have been coming here, ja?' asked Otto.

'Yeah, Gunther and that Ingrid girl.'

Ingrid and Gunther wait in front of apartment. 'Oh good, I am so glad we found you!' Ingrid says.

'We need you to speak again today,' says Gunther.

Ingrid shows me the placards she is carrying.

'I did not agree to any of this,' I say.

'Ohhhh...' Ingrid says as if the thought that I did not want to play along with her peace rally had not occurred to her. 'It's just that our work is so important.'

Inside I laugh at the urgent self-importance of youth.

'And you have so many good things to say.'

'Ja, you do.'

'Surely you can see the impact you had on people yesterday,' says Gunther.

'Just think of the impact you could have today. Even more people will attend tonight and hear your words.'

Skeptically, I look at Gunther and Ingrid. What is the American word for what these children are doing to me? *Shanghaied*, yes that is what is happening. I am being *Shanghaied* by an earnest young couple. So naïve and assuming that I would want to do as they ask. But I can see by the look in their eyes that they will be devastated if I turn them down.

'Very well,' I say. Their faces light up, their eyes shine. 'But this is the last time, do you hear?'

'Ja! Ja!'

The crowd is even larger than the previous day, running all the way down the street and spilling over into the side streets. In front of the podium is a television camera and crew.

'What is this?' I ask.

'I told the television station that you would be speaking and they sent this crew here. They will run excerpts of your speech during the news broadcast tonight.'

'How did you do all this?'

Gunther says, 'She hasn't slept in three days.'

Then I see deep bags under Ingrid's blood-shot eyes. 'You have to take care of yourself, my dear.'

'Ending this war is more important.'

Once more I am amazed at the energy and purpose of youth.

The crowd cheers as I take the podium. In minutes they are hanging on my every word, waiting for nuggets of wisdom from a man who is, in truth, just an old artist. While I see some polizei on the periphery of the crowd this time they do not dare try to break up the rally. There are simply too many people, and television cameras as well. A wise polizei commander has ordered his men to let events run their course.

When I finish, the crowd cheers and chants and waves German flags. The crowd slowly disperses singing Deutschland Über Alles.

'You nailed it!' Ingrid exclaims over the roar. 'You really nailed it!'

A man from the television crew comes forward. 'Good evening, mein Herr. I am a news producer and we would like to know if you would be willing to come to our studio for an interview.'

I do not say anything, but I see Ingrid, her face looking tired but hopeful. She knows that my appearing on television will be a great help to her movement. I admit I am intrigued by the idea of reaching so many people at once.

'Ja, I would like that very much.'

The producer gives me his card and says arrangements will be made for me to appear on television. I am to be at their studio at 3 PM.

'Three PM?' I ask. 'But your broadcast is not till seven?'

The producer laughs and says, 'We will pre-record the interview.'

'Ah,' I say.

At Ingrid's insistence she and Gunther take me to the studio. Partly, she wants to make sure I get there so her movement has its public spokesperson on television. But also, I know, they want to help an old man get to where he has to be. They are a nice young couple that way.

At the television station a guide shows me inside and takes me to a room just off the studio. Much to my surprise they put makeup on me. As an artist I understand how I need to look on camera so I do not resist, though the act is awkward. When makeup is finished the producer leads me onto the set. I sit in a small chair across from an interviewer. I recognize him from the television news. He introduces himself and explains the filming process to me. After I nod my understanding, he points to camera. A light comes on and he begins.

'So tell us about yourself.'

'I am seventy-five years old, born in Austria. I joined the Bavarian Army during the war and served in the 16th Reserve Infantry Regiment. I was on the western front but saw no fighting there. I saw much fighting in the east, though. Later I marched in the Kaiser's Grand Review of 1916.'

'And my producer tells me you were at the Grand Review this year.'

'Ja. I was with some American friends of mine and I watched the terror attack as it happened.

'American friends?'

'Ja my neighbors, a young woman and her six year old girl. Her husband works for the embassy here.'

'And you actually knew the attackers.'

'I would not say I knew the attackers. I would say I met and spoke with them at the Congo Pavilion a few days prior. I have travelled to Congo myself, though this was a long time ago, and was curious to meet two young Congolese.'

'Now what exactly did you say at that rally two days before? You are opposed to the war?'

'I would not say that. My position is much more complicated than merely being opposed to the war.'

'Then what do you say?'

'I say that the time has come for this war to stop.'

'But the French, the de Gaulle government has not yet been punished.'

'Nonsense,' I reply. 'Our forces occupy a wide swath of French territory.'

'But not Paris.'

'Is the goal of every war to occupy Paris?'

'Well...I...to punish the French...'

'And how many young German men must die to deliver this punishment? France has this new superweapon. It seems to be the stuff of nightmares, does it not? Men suffering and dying from the blast, still weeks after the blast. How many widows and orphans has this bomb made? What happens if France were to drop it on a German city? Why, the carnage would be enormous!'

'So what are you saying then, mein Herr?'

'We have generally beaten back the French Army. America and Britain are horrified with France's actions. Let us work with them to end the war and bring about a just peace.'

With that the interview ends.

We shake hands and the producer shows me out.

The next morning when I get to Weder's, Frau Weder is ecstatic. 'We received a letter from Tomas yesterday. He says he's stationed on the west bank of the Rhine and far away from all the trouble.'

'Thank goodness,' I say.

'And we saw you on the television last night.'

I cringe. Herr Weder must no doubt think badly of me.

He comes over to my table. 'I just want to shake your hand, mein Herr.'

In surprise I take his hand. 'Really?'

'I am so worried about my son and we were so thankful to hear he was on the Rhine rather than at the front.'

'Ja,' adds Frau Weder. 'We are just so scared that the French will unleash another one of those bombs of theirs.'

Herr Weder says, 'And what you said last night....' He shakes he head. 'No one can challenge a veteran like you.'

'Well thank you, both,' I say.

Frau Weder hands me the local paper and pours me a coffee. 'And it would seem you are having an effect.'

Veterans lead Peace March in Bremen, Köln... reads the headline. Accompanying the news is a photograph of an old, bespectacled veteran of the Great War. His uniform is ragged and moth ridden, but he marches in front of a demonstration of people. Men hold peace signs aloft.

Next to this a story proclaims, 'Polizei unsure what action to take....'

I read on. These are unlawful protests, for sure, and the polizei take a dim view of such gatherings. Usually these are broken up by riot police, mounted officers and tear gas. But veterans such as myself hold a special place in German society. Tear gassing veterans of the Great War would look bad, to say the least. Many young polizei are no doubt reluctant to do so anyway. We respect our elders in Germany.

'Excuse me, mein Herr,' a voice says.

I look up from my paper to see a pair of somewhat ragged youths standing on the street.

'We are sorry to bother you, but we saw you on television last night and just want to thank you.'

'Oh, no need to thank me.'

The two youths extend their hands, I shake each. 'We shall not bother you anymore. Good day, mein Herr.'

A moment later a passerby stops and then another, both point and look and cautiously approach me. By then, several people are standing on the sidewalk and murmuring amongst themselves.

'There he is!'

'I saw him on the television last night.'

'I cannot believe what he said.'

'He is completely right!'

I try to ignore the gawkers. But they are not to be dissuaded by my indifference. Eventually a polizei officer stops and wants to know why people are clogging up sidewalk traffic. He sees me and says, 'Oh, well then. Are you alright, mein Herr?'

'Ja, I am fine.'

'Come now, people!' the polizei shouts. 'Everyone move along. Move on now, go about your day.' He claps his hands. 'Move along!'

I smile and say, 'Thank you.'

'Not at all, mein Herr,' the polizei says. 'If you do not mind my saying, I enjoyed your television appearance last night.'

Two more people have stop and stare at me. 'I think it would be wise if you went home, mein Herr.'

'Ja, I believe you are right.'

That evening I hear a commotion outside of my window and see hundreds of young people walking past. The procession just keeps going until it is clear that tens of thousands are gathering at the Brandenburg gate. Later I hear a PA system and raucous cheering. Tens of thousands of voices combine to make an imposing roar. Aggie is ecstatic about the affair, positively beaming as she asks me, 'Do you hear!? Do you hear!?'

'Ja, I hear.'

'It is just like our own freedom marchers!'

More remarkable is the BBC Radio-1 news broadcast that night as relayed by Aggie. 'Oh, it so wonderful!' she recounts. 'The BBC reports that tens of thousands of young people have taken to the streets of Paris to protest this new bomb!'

'This would not be the first time the French have taken to the streets,' I say, much less impressed by the idea than Aggie is. 'In fact after the war…'

'They are demanding de Gaulle stop using the bomb!' Aggie is not to be dissuaded.

'That is good.'

'Don't you see what is happening?' Aggie demands.

'I am afraid…'

'It's the youth of the world coming to together!'

Far more important was the 'coming together' of the English and Americans, for the next morning I awoke to incredible news. In a joint communiqué, Prime Minister MacMillan and President Kennedy demand an immediate cessation of hostilities, assurances from de Gaulle that he will not use his new bombe atomique and the opening of negotiations under the auspices of a joint Anglo-American commission in Geneva. Prime Minister MacMillan spoke first from London saying that Her Majesty's government was prepared to use military force to prevent France from using the bombe atomique again. De Gaulle issues a defiant communiqué himself, vowing the French people would never bend their knee to 'les Anglos'.

But later in the day President Kennedy announces that the United States will support and participate in any military action the British deem necessary to prevent the use of le bombe atomique. As I listen, I wonder what Aggie would think of her president after this announcement. Later that day Bob actually comes home. He seems exhausted but wants to talk at dinner.

'Just what, exactly, is the president going to do?' Aggie asks.

Bob sips his wine and breathes deeply. 'He's not messing around. He's ordered a carrier battlegroup to sail out of Norfolk and join the British blockade. And he's flying fighter and bomber aircraft to Iceland.'

'He is serious then,' I say.

'He is. Already some people in the senate are screaming bloody murder,' Bob says wearily.

'Who could oppose such a thing?' Aggie asks.

'The isolationist types. Lodge, Taft, Miller and the like. A few others are talking about our historic link with France. The whole Democratic party is going along, though. The president owns them, after all.'

'Like Speer and the conservatives,' I nod.

'This is only the right thing to do,' Aggie says.

I smile at her naïveté and ask Bob, 'Do you really think the United States will go to war?'

Bob takes a bite and replies, 'That I can't say. But this certainly brings a lot of pressure on France, no?' Bob shakes his head. 'Unless Russia steps in,

France is finished. She's looking at the combined might of Germany, the UK and the USA.'

'But that bomb of theirs…' says Aggie.

'How many of those things can they have?' Bob asks. 'And now that we know these bombs can be made…'

'Oh no,' Aggie says.

'Yes,' Bob replies. 'Word from friends back at Foggy Bottom is the president will request a billion dollars in emergency research funding next month.'

'That's horrible!' Aggie says. 'If everyone has these bombs…' She looks at her Erica, who is happily eating her dinner and making construction noises with her fork.

'One thing at a time,' Bob says. 'For now we are ending this stupid war.'

I look at Aggie and say, 'He is right, you know. For now we are getting peace.' For a moment I think back to my service fifty years earlier. 'And that is a good thing.'

'Oh!' Bob says to me. 'I should tell you, you're something of a sensation in Washington. They've seen your television appearances.'

'Have they really?' I ask.

'Yes, and President Kennedy asked me about you; who is this Adolph Hitler?'

Old Hitler, by Shourabh Mukherji

America fought three existential conflicts. The First World War was not one of them. That war is sandwiched between our own Civil War, and the Second World War. Both swallow the Great War's history and memory. Americans don't often appreciate the importance of the Great War. That terrible, useless conflict is the most important event in European history since the Fall of the Roman Empire. The war changed the course of history and lay the groundwork for our own wretched and miserable 20th century.

Without the First World War, or if Germany wins early on as it does in *The Austrian Painter*, the 20th century changes beyond all recognition. Without the First World War there is no Second World War, obviously, but also no communist revolution in Russia. The Russian Empire need not endure the pressures brought on by the war, and Germany would have had no need to send V.I. Lenin to Russia. There is no Mao, no Pol Pot. There is no Manhattan Project, no space program-no space race. In short, the Austrian Painter's 1964 is unrecognizable to us.

What came in *The Austrian Painter* is, we think, a likely scenario for what that world would have been like. A powerful Germany lies in the heart of Europe. The Reich still has a Kaiser, though the institution's power is lessening. Germany possesses an important colonial empire, a strong second in power and prestige to the British Empire.

In *The Austrian Painter* the British Empire sits astride the world. The First World War broke Great Britain, financially, physically, and morally. The 1916 disaster on the Somme drained that nation of its energy and confidence. Britain has never recovered. But in *The Austrian Painter* there is no Somme and no Second World War to bankrupt the empire. The Dominions have no need to turn to America for leadership. Britain has the wherewithal to withstand the Indian independence push.

In the world of *The Austrian Painter* after a long war in the Pacific, the American experience at home is not much different than in our world, and the social forces at work in our 1964 are at work in the Austrian Painter's 1964. Here it is supposed Joe Kennedy didn't get killed, and little brother John has no path to the White House. Also, did anyone catch the brief reference to Eisenhower at MacArthur's funeral?

Otherwise we decided not to get cute. The Austrian Painter never stumbles upon Herr Goering or befriends Herr Hesse at Otto's. We suspect the reader was on the lookout for such tricks. Of course Albert Speer is the Chancellor. We went this way for two reasons. We wanted someone recognizable for the spot (who in America has ever heard of Willie Brandt?). Second Speer rose through Nazi ranks. Why could not have done the same in a mid-20th century Imperial Germany?

So now we come to it. Why interpret this alternate age through the eyes of Adolph Hitler? Some readers probably found this book discomforting or controversial. A few Hitler fan bois probably enjoyed this book for all the wrong reasons. As the First World War made the 20th century, so it made Adolph Hitler. In 1914 Hitler was an art school reject supporting himself through commissioned landscape paintings and postcards. There is little to indicate he had strong opinions about Jews or anything else political before the war. Like most of the German Army in 1918, Hitler felt hurt and betrayed by the Berlin politicos, stabbed in the back, as the saying goes. This led to feelings of rage and the formation of his National Socialist ideology. We say again the Hitler of 1914 was not the raging, hate filled warmonger of 1933.

In researching Hitler we started with Vulker Ullrich's *Hitler: Ascent, 1889-1939.* Ullrich gives one a sense of the man and his origins. For his time in the First World War we relied upon Thomas Weber's excellent *Hitler's First*

War. This work tells us not only about Hitler, but the entire 16th Bavarian Reserve Infantry Regiment including the characters seen here. Hitler made friends other than Ernst Schmidt, but most of them came later in the war. We left them out as to not crowd the chapter. As for Hitler's tastes we relied on two works, both fascinating. Hitler and the Power of Aesthetics by Frederic Spotts talks about the Reich's use of Neo-Classical, Brutalist architecture to create a physical manifestation of the imposing and all-knowing state that was everywhere yet untouchable. Despina Stratigakos' Hitler at Home is about, well, Hitler at home, his taste in architecture and décor.

Overall researching The Austrian Painter was interesting and writing it quite satisfying. We thank our editor, Debbie Jaeger for her keen eye and our proofers Lee and Sharon Moyer. Any errors remaining are the author's own. As always thanks to the reader for coming this far, your presence is felt. Those interested may look us up on Facebook, visit WilliamStroock.blogspot.com, or follow us on Gab.ai.

Made in the USA
San Bernardino, CA
30 December 2018